Rover

Rover

JACKIE FRENCH

HARPERCOLLINS*PUBLISHERS*

Library of Congress Cataloging-in-Publication Data is available.
ISBN-10: 0-06-085078-7 (trade bdg.) — ISBN-13: 978-0-06-085078-4 (trade bdg.)
ISBN-10: 0-06-085079-5 (lib. bdg.) — ISBN-13: 978-0-06-085079-1 (lib. bdg.)

Typography by Al Cetta

1 2 3 4 5 6 7 8 9 10
❖
First U.S. edition, 2007

To Lily,
a dog of total loyalty
and perfect manners

Contents

Prologue

1. Hekja

2. The Rescue

3. The Problem of Food

4. Up the Great Mountain

5. A Hunter at Last

6. Danger on the Mountain

7. A Song for a Hero!

8. Raiders!

9. Attack!

10. The Ship

11. Under Sail

12. Storm

13. The Iceberg

14. Out from the Fog

15. Land of Snow

16. The New Home

17. Greenland

18. Strange Ships

19. The Traders

20. The Race

21. Mist!

22. A Feast and a Challenge

23. A Greenland Winter

24. Yule Feast

25. A Hero's Farewell

26. After the Funeral

27. Freydis's Followers

28. Leaving Greenland

29. The Journey

30. Land!

31. The First Night in Vinland

32. Exploring Vinland

33. The Skraelings

34. The Skraelings Arrive

35. Vinland Days

36. Winter Feasting

37. The Attack!

38. After the Raid

39. A Child Is Born

40. Finnbogi

41. A Decision

42. The Battle

43. The Death of Honor

44. Leaving Vinland

45. A Song for Freydis

Author's Note

GREENLAND

NORTH AMERICA

× × ×

● Bratthalid

ATLANTIC

NEW FOUNDLAND

— — — possible route taken by Freydis to Vinland

.... route from Denmark to Bratthalid, in which Hekja was captured

× × × Hekja and Hikki's run

Printer move legend 3/4" to right

ICELAND

NORWAY

SWEDEN

OCEAN

ENGLAND

Prologue

When a witch gives you a True Name, it sticks.

The witch was called Tikka, and she lived at the foot of the tallest mountain on the island. It was Tikka you'd go to for spiderwebs to staunch a cut or crushed black snails to cure a spider bite.

The witch had come to the chief's hut that day because the chief's youngest son had cut his foot on a clamshell. Even the witch came when the chief ordered.

He wasn't much of a chief, just lord of a cluster of stone huts that stood by the bay. Nor was his hut much, either. It was round, like the other huts in the village, dug deep down into the rocky soil, so the lower-half walls were dirt and the upper parts were rocks all fitted together, with a cowhide across the doorway and a smoke hole above the fireplace.

The chief had sent his oldest son, Bran, to fetch the witch, and the witch had hobbled down from her hut and had bound up the boy's foot with a scrap of soft leather dipped in crushed shell and her own urine, muttering all the time so that the chief and his wife would think that she was wise.

Once the wound was bound and the boy had stopped sniveling, the witch accepted a horn of ale and a barley cake with cheese and looked around the hut.

A witch doesn't ask for a fee. People give what they like, but if you don't give her what she wants, a storm will blow up next time your man is out fishing and the sea will have his bones. Or that was what the witch hoped you would think.

There wasn't much to see inside the hut—just the peat fire glowing and the iron pot simmering with stew for the evening, the fish hung up from the rafters to dry, and the chief's fine hunting dog[1] with all her little puppies crawling round her lying in the corner by the hearth.

"Would you name the puppies for us, Tikka?" asked the chief's wife.

Old Tikka laughed and picked up one of the puppies. It growled, and tried to lick her nose. "I'll call this one Courage," she said.

"That's the dog for me then," said Bran boastfully. He was the tallest boy in the village, and the strongest, with thick brown plaits to his waist. His father had promised him the pick of the litter.

---

[1] The dogs of this time were giant, long-legged dogs, the ancestors of Scottish wolfhounds or deerhounds.

The witch picked up another puppy and held her up so she could see her in the light from the open doorway. "Ah, a fine bitch this," she said approvingly. "I'll call her Faithful Long Legs. May she always . . ."

That's when it happened.

It was the smallest pup of all, the one with the fattest stomach and the longest ears, feet the size of barley cakes and a nose that looked like it had been stubbed on the floor. He'd been suckling his mother long after the others finished, and there was milk dribbled all down his front.

He toddled a step or two, just far enough so he didn't widdle in the bed, then crouched and let fly.

The witch let out a yell and lifted up her foot, all wet and dripping.

Bran chuckled and so did the chief, though he stopped when Tikka glared at him. Even the chief wouldn't cross a hag. His wife raced up with some soft cowhide and mopped Tikka's foot. The witch put the bitch down and picked up the other pup by the scruff of his neck.

"Arf arf arf," he barked, sending a spray of milk all over the witch's face.

Tikka stared at the puppy thoughtfully. "As for you," she said, "I'll call you . . ." She grinned, showing her long white teeth. "I'll call you Riki Snarfari," she decided. And with that she put him down.

Bran let out a yell. "Riki Snarfari.[2] That pup will

[2] literally Mighty Sailor, or Rover, who travels fast

never be a mighty rover! He's the laziest pup of the litter!"

The witch held his eye. "Are you arguing with me, boy?"

Bran subsided. "No, Tikka," he muttered.

Riki Snarfari, the Mighty Rover, crawled back to his mother's side and tried to hide his head under her warmth. He peered out at the witch, who was filling up her second cup of ale and accepting the best of the barley cakes.

The witch saw him peering at her and laughed.

Chapter 1

Hekja

Hekja sat on her rock by the shore and let her eyes follow the clouds floating on the far horizon. Pa had once sung a song about a land of cloud, where fish swam through the air and jewels grew on the trees.

Hekja wasn't sure what jewels were—a type of cheese, perhaps—for Pa had died before she could ask him. But every time the clouds hung on the horizon, Hekja remembered Pa's island. One day, she thought, when I am married, I'll ask my husband to sail his boat out to the horizon. We'll step out onto the cloud land and pick the jewels. . . .

Hekja smiled to herself and picked up her cockle[3] stick again. At this rate the tide would be in before she had her basket half full.

Then she saw the puppy.

He was the smallest dog Hekja had ever seen, and for such a small thing, he had the fattest belly. It almost dragged along the pebbles as he stumbled

---

[3]shellfish that live in the sand

1

from the chief's hut down to the shore.

Hekja put down her bag of shellfish and watched the pup toddle across the salty, damp stones, sniffing as he went until he found a dead seal pup, half buried in a drift of seaweed, with the waves lapping just below.

None of the village folk ate seals—too many of their families, they said, were descended from seal ancestors. Which meant rich and meaty as this seal was, no one had come to eat it.

Hekja watched as the puppy nuzzled at the seal, trying to find a way in to the good meat. But the furry sealskin was too tough for his small jaws and tiny milk teeth. He was almost ready to give up when he found a soft patch, where the skin had rotted through. . . .

"Craaaarrrrk!" A seagull swooped above.

The pup paid no attention.

"Carwwkkk!" The seagull was closer now, and angry. It wanted that seal for itself.

"Grrr," snarled the puppy warningly, lifting up his tiny nose.

"Keeerk!" shrieked the bird. It flew at the pup and pecked his eye.

The puppy screamed. The bird pecked again, this time at the pup's leg and rounded stomach, and then once more at his eyes. The pup tried to stumble away, his hurt leg dragging behind him. He could hardly see because of the blood.

Hekja grabbed a stone and threw it as hard as she could. "Get away from him!" The bird gave a startled squawk and flapped away. The puppy cowered, whimpering, by the drifts of seaweed.

Hekja ran toward him, her shellfish forgotten, and picked him up carefully. Blood welled from above his eye, and his torn leg dangled limply. The puppy yelped with pain.

"Let me see!" It was the chief. He grabbed the pup by the scruff of the neck. The puppy yelped louder as the chief's hand pulled at his injured leg.

"He's lamed and blinded. Stupid animal, he's good for nothing now." The chief's voice was angry. The pup had been worth a good calf, or more. "He's not worth feeding. There's only one thing for him . . ." said the chief as his hands closed around the puppy's throat.

"No!" Hekja's voice was high and fierce. "You can't kill him!"

The chief stared at her. "He's mine. I can do what I like with him."

"I'll look after him! Please! I'll make him better!"

"Pa?" It was Bran. He must have been watching from the hut. "Let Hekja have the pup if she wants it. It's no good to us."

The chief paused, then dumped the puppy in Hekja's arms.

The pup had stopped whimpering now and was limp and still. Was he dead already?

The chief shrugged. "Keep him then. He's done for anyway." He turned and stamped off up the shore.

Chapter 2

The Rescue

Hekja ran along the shore to the hut she shared with her mother. Once there had been five of them in the hut. But Hekja's brothers had been drowned when a storm raged across the islands, and Pa's back had been broken when he'd fallen from the cliff when the men were collecting eggs. So now it was just Hekja and her ma.

Ma sat in the doorway, grinding the barley flour for their meal. She stared at the bloody bundle in Hekja's arms. "What in all the islands is that?!" she exclaimed.

"It's a puppy! He's hurt. Ma, please! Please let me keep him!"

Her ma stood and peered at the puppy, then shook her head. "He's hurt too bad, love."

"I'll look after him! I'll make him well!"

Her ma picked up the quern[4] of barley flour and began to mix it with water to be baked on the hearth-stone for dinner. "He'll die and break your heart,"

---

[4] a stone bowl used for grinding grain

she said softly. "And even if he lives, what would we feed him? Barley bread and fish heads? There is little enough for ourselves."

Hekja stroked the puppy silently. Finally her ma said, "You know what it was like with your pa, after his accident. It's not easy, love, tending someone you love, watching him die."

"I know," whispered Hekja. "But I can't just leave him. I have to try to make him well."

Hekja's ma bit her lip. Then she nodded. "All right. You can try."

"Could you fetch Tikka for him? Please, Ma!"

The woman's voice was firm now. "Tikka would need rewarding. I'll not be asking her to come all this way, just for a pup that won't last the night."

"Then I'll take him to her myself!"

"Hekja, love . . ." pleaded her ma. Then she bit her lip. "If you will."

It was cold outside. Hekja hugged the puppy close, and began to run.

Hekja was good at running. She'd had a lot of practice, chasing the cow as it nosed after pasture and running down to the fishing boats to beg for scraps. Sometimes she ran along the pebbles of the bay when there was no one else to see, just for the joy of running. She pretended that if she ran fast enough, she could catch the sunset.

But this run was different. There was no time to enjoy the wind in her face. The scent of the sea changed to cattle smells and heather as she neared the witch's home. The puppy whimpered in her arms, and then was still.

Tikka's hut sat by the burn[5] that bubbled down from the snow-melt great mountain. The witch had lived by herself as long as Hekja could remember, picking her herbs by moonlight, when their magic was the strongest, muttering her curses if the men forgot to bring her share of fish, or if the chief was late bringing his bull to her cow. Today the witch's cow was grazing across the burn, near to calving. It stared at Hekja, then bent its head to the grass.

Hekja paused by the cowhide door. She'd just have called and gone in to any other hut. But no one entered Tikka's uninvited. Hekja caught her breath, then called as politely as she could, "Tikka, please, it's Hekja. I have a puppy. He's hurt."

The tattered cowhide moved, and the witch's face emerged. She looked at the pup and grinned. No other woman the witch's age had all her teeth, but Tikka's were long and white. The other girls said Tikka had once charmed them from a wolf, up on the great mountain.

"Ah, that one, is it?" said Tikka, the toothy grin pushing the wrinkles on her face into new patterns. "Riki Snarfari, the Mighty Rover. I knew that he'd be trouble."

"Riki Snarfari?" Hekja glanced at the pup doubt-

---

[5] small stream

fully. He didn't look like a mighty anything.

"Named him myself. It's a True Name." The witch stepped out of her hut, bringing with her the scent of fish oil and old herbs, and just a breath of barley beer. She lifted the pup's nose, then twisted his leg. The puppy howled in pain.

"Will he die?" whispered Hekja.

"Yes," said Tikka. And then she cackled, just like a witch should, and the smell of herbs and beer became stronger. "But not for many years yet! Bring him inside, girl, and let's see to him."

Hekja hesitated. "I have nothing for you."

"You have your legs, girl," said Tikka. "You'll be taking my cow up the mountain with the others in summer. Now bring him inside."

It was dark in the hut, with the hide across the doorway blocking out the spring sunlight. A pot bubbled on the smouldering turf fire underneath the smoke hole. Hekja blinked at it. "Those look like . . . snails. . . ."

The witch peered at her, then cackled again. "Most girls would scream at a pot of snails. Nothing wrong with snails, girl. Cook them with their shells and mush the lot and eat them once a week and you'll have teeth as good as mine, no matter how many babies your husband gives you."

"The girls said you have wolf teeth." Hekja could have grabbed the words back, but the witch just grinned, her white teeth glowing in the dimness. "I'm happy they think so, so don't go telling them otherwise. But they're my own, every one of them. How'd I get wolf teeth to stay in? Now, let's see this pup. How did you end up with him?"

"I rescued him. The chief said I could have him."

"Generous. Bet he'll wish he hadn't when the pup gets bigger."

Hekja felt her heart pound louder than the bubbling burn. "Then he'll recover?"

Tikka nodded. She laid the puppy on the stone bench, and he whimpered with the cold and the pain of being moved. "The eye's bad," she muttered. "Nothing we can do about that, except help it heal." She bent down and sniffed Snarf's blood-stained stomach. "Can't smell guts, so nothing's punctured. That's how you can tell how bad a wound is, girl. If you can smell guts, then there's no hope."

"Will he be able to walk?" said Hekja anxiously.

"He might limp a bit. But his bones are still soft because he's young, so they should heal. Aye, he'll recover, if you care for him enough."

"I will," promised Hekja.

The witch stirred up the turf fire. She poured the boiled snails into a wood jar and refilled the pot with water from the bucket by the door. Next she selected herbs from the long lines drying from the roof and threw them into the water to heat.

"See? You'll have to do this, too." She thrust the

herbs at Hekja's nose. "Smell! Think you can find those again?"

Hekja nodded. "Yes. That's wild garlic and that—"

"I know what they are, girl! As long as you do too. Now, cook them for as long as it takes to sing two verses of the "Fisherman's Lament." Wait for the potion to cool and wash him with it. Then mix the herbs with honey to cover up the wounds. You've got honey at home?"

Hekja shook her head. The witch sighed. "There's a pot of it behind the door. Take it. But this autumn you seek out a hive, mind, and pay me back."

"I will," promised Hekja.

"Mind you don't burn him—the herbs should be hot. And you bandage him like this, just firm enough to hold. Change the dressing twice a day," instructed Tikka, "until the wounds start to scab, then leave them clear."

"What about the magic?" asked Hekja timidly. "Don't I have to say words over him or something?"

Tikka laughed. It was a real laugh, not her witch's cackle. "The power's in the herbs, not me. Magic is good to trick the foolish into doing what they should have done if they'd had sense in the first place. Though sometimes . . ." The witch paused suddenly and frowned. "Hekja . . ."

"Yes, Tikka?"

"Tell your ma this dog will be useful. He'll be worth the feeding. Tell her you'll be needing him."

"To help watch the cows?"

"For that, too," said the witch cryptically. "Now be off with you."

Hekja nodded. She lifted the pup carefully and kissed his nose. "Come on, Riki Snarfari, my little Snarf. We're going home."

Chapter 3

The Problem of Food

That night Hekja slept on her bracken bed with Snarf beside her. She kept him warm with her cowhide cover, and when he whimpered she held him closer.

The next morning she changed the bandages. The pup whined, especially when she pulled off the herbs. But when she had finished he snuggled close again.

Her ma peered through the door. She'd been dragging the wood plough through the rocky soil outside the hut so they could plant the spring kale and barley seed. Normally Hekja would have helped, but today she was staying close to Snarf.

"How is he?"

"I think he's stronger," said Hekja hopefully. "Aren't you, Snarf?"

"Arf arf!" said the puppy weakly.

Hekja laughed. "He knows his name!"

Her ma smiled. "Riki Snarfari! What a name for a pup like that! You should call him Cuddles, or Wimperwail."

Hekja shook her head stubbornly. "Tikka says his name is Riki Snarfari. She says it's a True Name and that he'll be useful."

Her ma opened her mouth to speak, but when she saw the happiness on Hekja's face, she shut it again. Happiness came too rarely to the hut on the shore since their men had died. So she said instead, "You need to feed him something."

Hekja nodded. She put the puppy on her lap and held a handful of warm barley mash up to his nose. Snarf whined and held his nose away.

"He won't eat," said Hekja despairingly.

"He's too small, perhaps," said her ma. "He's forgotten how to lap, if he ever knew it. Here." She lifted Snarf's chin with one hand and gently edged the tips of two fingers in his mouth. A trickle of the barley mash was down his throat before he even realized it. "My gran showed me that for a poorly calf," said Hekja's ma. "You try it."

Snarf swallowed a few mouthfuls, then seemed to realize what was happening. He shut his jaws and tried to squirm away.

Hekja's ma shook her head. "Dogs like meat," she said quietly.

Hekja said nothing. The hut had no smoked legs of meat hanging from its rafters. Even fish was precious.

When Hekja looked up, Bran was standing at the door.

"How is the pup doing?"

"He won't eat," said Hekja worriedly. "And we don't have any meat to give him."

Hekja had caught him looking at her lately when he thought she wasn't looking. Sometimes she looked at him as well. Nothing could ever come of it, she knew, even if she had been old enough to think of marriage. A chief's son should marry another chief's daughter, who could bring a herd of cattle and a year's worth of cheeses to her husband.

Bran shrugged. "Too bad," he said carelessly. A moment later, he was gone.

But later, when Snarf was sleeping, Bran reappeared and thrust something through the door.

"Here. See if he'll eat that," he said. He was gone before Hekja could thank him.

Hekja looked at what he'd brought. It was a badger, limp and bloody.

Suddenly the pup lifted up his head. "Arf!" he announced weakly.

Hekja laughed. "You like the smell of badger meat, do you! Thank you!" she called to Bran. But there was no reply.

Hekja's ma cooked the badger with the barley, to make the meat go further. Hekja trickled the mush into Snarf's mouth, as she had done before. At first he ate reluctantly, but soon he began to gobble, as though he had realized he was hungry. Afterward Hekja held him on her knee and scratched carefully behind his ear, so as not to disturb his wounds.

She sang a song her father had taught her, and that his father had sung too, mending the fishing nets, or at the summer feast. The villagers had said Pa's voice was so beautiful, even the seals came to shore to hear it. This was the first time Hekja had sung since he died.

"Wind on the river,
Wind on the sea,
There the wind rests,
and my love rests with me."

Her ma smiled as she ground the barley in the quern for the night's barley cake. Then suddenly Snarf lifted up his nose.

"Hooooooooowwwwwwwl!!!!!"

Hekja's ma laughed. "He's saying, 'No, this is how you sing properly!'"

Hekja looked down at the pup. He was so small, and so earnest. She bent down to rub her nose on his. But by now the pup was nearly asleep.

* * *

Bran brought meat every few days after that. One day there was hare, and then a squirrel, and sometimes a puffin or a cod head. Occasionally, he even brought scraps of venison from the chief's table. Hekja knew he was busy fishing with the men each day and that he must have spent all his nights up on the great mountain, setting his snares for her. But he just handed the bloody lumps to her through the door, as though the gift was nothing.

Snarf grew stronger day by day. He ate barley cake now too, with cheese and sour butter and smoked fish, the same food that Hekja and her mother ate.

Before long he was well enough to limp after Hekja as she collected shellfish or seaweed. His fat belly almost dragged on the ground as he nosed at the fish guts by the smoking barrels that were dug into the pebbly shore. He bounced at the waves and dug in the village compost heap till he stunk of rotten kale stems and dung.

Day by day Snarf's leg got better, so that soon he hardly limped at all, except when he was tired.

Sometimes Hekja felt the chief's eyes upon her as she threw driftwood for Snarf to chase on the stony shore. Snarf might limp, and his face was scarred, but he was still a valuable dog, worth three sacks of barley at least, or a cow.

But Snarf was Hekja's now.

The days grew longer. The men went after gulls' eggs, and there were eggs enough for everyone, even Hekja's hut on the shore. For weeks the whole village smelled of egg farts, and Snarf's belly looked round as an egg itself.

And then it was summer, the longer days eating up the night and the midges biting every bit of skin they could find. Above the village the great mountain turned from white to brown to green.

It was time to take the cattle up to pasture.

Chapter 4

Up the Great Mountain

Taking the cattle to pasture was a task for the girls of the village. The men and boys fished, hunted, mended the fishing nets, and cut the turf for burning. The women dried the fish in long flapping lines outside the round stone huts; they planted the barley and the kale in the rocky soil, then ground the grain to flour for the barley cakes. They made the barley beer[6] and collected shellfish and driftwood along the shore.

The bull calves stayed in the chef's enclosure to be butchered for meat, but every summer the village girls took the shaggy high-horned cows and calves up the mountain to get fat on fresh new grass. They milked the cows and made the butter and the cheese.

Twice each moon the women made the journey up the mountain to bring the girls fish and barley cakes, to check the goings-on, and to collect the soft new cheese. Then they would carry it back down to the vil-

---

[6] a very low-alcohol beer, more like ginger beer than the beers we drink today

16

lage to press the cheese, and bury the butter in the cold, wet soil by the stream, so it would still be fresh to eat in winter when the cows no longer gave their milk.

This was the first year that Hekja was to go. She had twelve summers now, and would be the youngest of them all.

The whole village gathered to see them off, including Bran, who stared at Hekja then pretended that he wasn't. The cows were all garlanded with wild flowers, which the calves kept chewing off until the cows mooed, to keep them in line. They could smell the new grass up the mountainside. Snarf leaped around them all, snapping at their heels. He seemed to know he was the only dog going up the mountain. No other girl in the village had a dog. Dogs were for men.

The women carried the wooden pails for the milk, the butter paddles, and the cheese cloths. The girls carried their bundles, barley cakes and dried fish, and cowhide blankets to keep them warm, for even summer nights were cold up on the mountain. There were five of them: Raina and Reena, the chief's two daughters and the oldest of the girls; Janna from the hut beyond the bay; Banna, Hekja's best friend who lived in a hut nearby; and Hekja.

Hekja's ma had only one cow, with its calf at foot, while the chief had ten. The village would divy the cheese and butter up, a certain amount for each cow you owned, with extra for the families of the girls who'd looked after the cows up on the mountain.

Snarf was half grown now, with the long legs of his mother and a coat as shaggy as a cow's.

The cows were slow and the calves kept trying to suckle their mothers, but the air was sweet with summer, so no one was in any hurry. Finally they reached the mountain meadows and the sheiling[7] where the girls would sleep and keep the milk cool. It was no bigger than the huts down by the shore; made of stone with a dirt floor, but no fireplace, as there was no wood to burn up here on the mountain.

While the girls laid down their bundles, the women set up the buckets and the butter paddles, then cut turfs to mend the holes in the roof. Then the girls began to gather bracken for their beds and watercress for their lunch.

Some of the women were tearful at the of leaving their daughters. But the girls were exultant. After four summers of milking, you were judged a woman, and could marry. You could even use some of the cheeses you made up on the mountain for your dowry.

It was time for the women to go. Hekja hugged her ma extra hard. The other women had husbands and other family to go back to, but Hekja's ma had no one else. Even her cow was on the mountain.

"Take care," whispered Hekja's ma.

Hekja nodded. "I will. You take care too."

---

[7] a summer hut

Her mother smiled. "What can happen to me down in the village?" But her look was one of longing as she gazed at Hekja and touched her cheek for one last time. "Take care of her, Riki Snarfari," she instructed Snarf.

"Arf," said Snarf, sitting on Hekja's foot and panting. He'd already rolled in fresh cow dung and looked proud of his new smell.

"See?" said Hekja. "He understands!" But her ma just smiled and bit her lip, then followed the other women down the path.

Hekja stood watching her, till the path twisted and she was out of sight. Then she turned back to the sheiling.

The other girls were already inside, setting out their bedding. As the chief's daughters, Raina and Reena took charge. Reena pointed to the back of the hut, furthest from the draught of the door. "We'll sleep there," she said.

"And you'll sleep there," Raina said to Hekja, pointing to the windy spot by the entrance. The chief's daughters weren't fond of Hekja for her dress was ragged hide, not woven wool like theirs, and their brother liked her far too much.

"And the dog can sleep outside," said Reena. "What's he doing here, anyway?"

Hekja said nothing, just set her chin in the stubborn way her ma said was just like her father, when he meant to do something but didn't care to argue about it. She was quite happy to sleep by the door, and when the girls were asleep Snarf could slip in beside her, just as he did at home.

She smiled in spite of the chief's daughters. You could see the whole world from up here, she thought, the islands scattered across the sea and the line where the waves met the sky. And she had Snarf, too. What did it matter what Raina and Reena said?

It was time for milking. The cows were tired after their walk, and there was not much milk tonight, as the calves had been drinking all day. Tomorrow the girls would keep the calves away from the cows, so they'd eat the soft new grass instead of sucking at their mothers. The milk supply would be better.

The girls put the buckets of milk in the hut for the cream to rise, but kept one bucketful for their dinner.

They sat on the cool grass as the last of the sunlight drained away across the sea. The chief's daughters drank first, then passed the bucket around, each girl drinking her fill. Hekja was the last. It was rich milk tonight too, with all the cream still in it. When she finished, she passed the bucket to Snarf. He'd just got his tongue into the milk when someone snatched the bucket away.

It was Reena. "The milk is not for dogs!"

"I'll wash the bucket clean over in the spring," said Hekja mildly.

"Why should we share the milk with your dog?" said Janna angrily. "If the chief's daughters don't have a dog, why should you?"

Janna, too, had been casting glances at Bran, down in the village.

"Snarf can have half my share."

"He stinks," said Raina.

"It's a good smell! It's a dog smell!" said Hekja hotly. She grabbed Snarf and hugged him close to her. Snarf licked her face happily and grinned at the girls, his long tongue hanging out.

"He stinks of cow shush," said Raina.

"And fish guts," said Reena.

Hekja said nothing. It was true. Snarf had been nosing in the compost heap just that morning.

"Arf!" said Snarf, looking at the girls with whiskery friendliness and licking his milk moustache.

It didn't work. "Let him hunt his own food," said Reena.

"But he's lame!" pleaded Hekja. "And he's still too young to hunt!" It hadn't occurred to her that the girls on the mountain wouldn't share with Snarf as she and her mother had done.

Reena shrugged. "Then he's not worth his keep," she said. "Anyway, dogs belong in tthe village with the men."

Hekja looked at Banna, her friend, hoping for support. But Banna just looked at the grass.

Hekja bit her lip, then fumbled in her bundle for her barley bread and cheese. "Here, boy," she whispered.

Snarf gulped the bread and cheese in two large bites, then looked for more. Hekja shook her head and tried to ignore the hunger clawing at her stomach.

The starlight lit the mountain cliffs with silver as they went to bed. Hekja listened to the talk slowly cease and the girls' breathing soften.

"Snarf!" she whispered.

He had been just around the corner, sitting puzzled in the dark. He stretched out beside her and licked her face, scratched his ear twice where a grass seed was prickling, then laid his paws on his nose.

Hekja lay awake. It was strange to lie in a new place, the familiar sound of waves lapping on the pebbles replaced with the noises of the other girls sleeping and the cows mooing in the night.

How could Snarf learn to hunt, with no one to show him how, and one lame leg? He wasn't even fully grown.

Perhaps she could sneak him some of the milk tomorrow. If he ate nothing, he'd be too weak to hunt, but If he was just a little hungry, he might decide to hunt himself.

* * *

By the next morning, the cream had risen to the top of the milk. The girls scooped it off into the butter pail and, like the night before, passed the pail around, drinking as much as they wanted of the cold skimmed milk. Snarf watched, looking hopeful.

Hekja gave him a bit of her barley cake, while the girls looked on and snickered. There wasn't much barley cake left—the girls only had a bite or two to go with their milk and watercress, and the dried fish and cheese finished too. Soon they'd have fresh cheese to eat, and buttermilk, but there would be no more barley cake till the women came up again.

Hekja bit her lip. A big dog like Snarf needed food every day—lots of food, as he was still growing.

Reena dusted off the last of the crumbs and took a final drink of milk. "Now," she ordered. "Hekja, you churn the butter while we watch the cows."

Hekja said nothing. Butter making was harder work than sitting watching the cows and yelling at them when they strayed. But if she was alone at the sheiling, she could give Snarf some of the cream.

She sat in the sheiling's doorway on a three-legged stool, with the bucket between her knees, and swept the butter paddles back and forth in the cream. She waited for the cows—and the girls—to wander off.

But the cows stayed where they were. There was plenty of grass by the sheiling, and their legs were tired from yesterday.

Hekja glanced down at Snarf, sleeping at her feet, with one eye half open to check on the cows. "Please go and hunt, Snarf. Please," she whispered.

Snarf glanced up at her. He seemed quite content to wait for breakfast, whenever Hekja would get around to getting it. After all, she had always provided for him before. He put his head back on his paws and shut his eyes.

Hekja bit her lip. If she had been a boy, she'd have learned to hunt with the men. She'd be able to teach Snarf to hunt too. *Maybe I should take him back to the chief,* she thought hopelessly. *Maybe Bran will take him. . . .*

The day stretched out. Hekja drank some of the skimmed milk with the other girls as the sun rose in the sky, and packed the first of the summer's butter into the butter crock, with its tight-fitting lid to keep out dust and flies—and Snarf's nose.

Snarf looked hopefully from girl to girl as they drank. When the bucket was empty, he whined and looked questioningly at Hekja. But she just shook her head. "I'm sorry," she whispered.

Tomorrow, I'll take him to Bran tomorrow.

Chapter 5

A Hunter at Last

Hekja woke in the night to Reena's gentle snores. Snarf was not at her side. Where is he? Had he wandered off in the night? Was he heading back to the village where he knew he would be fed? Maybe he'd had an accident! Fallen down a cliff like Pa . . . or maybe a wolf had caught him . . .

The moon rose above the ridge like a small yellow cheese.

Hekja sat up. She had to find Snarf! She had to!

She crept from the hut, then called softly into the darkness, "Snarf! Riki Snarfari!"

No answer. She walked a little further and called again, "Snarf! Snarf!"

Suddenly something bounded out of the darkness. "Arf," said Snarf softly, bulling her with his furry head. Then he leaped into the darkness again, turning his head back as though to say, "Are you coming?"

Hekja followed him. The moonlight cast shadows on the grass as Snarf began to run. Hekja tied her skirts about her waist and ran, too. It was hard at first avoiding the clumps of heather. But as the moon rose higher, it grew easier. If she looked at the ground, Hekja discovered, and not the moonlit sky, her eyes grew used to the dimness.

Hekja could feel hunger nibble at her tummy. And if she was hungry, what must Snarf feel like? Then suddenly she stopped, as still as the mountain crags about them. He sniffed, then crept forward, his nose to the ground.

Hekja froze. What had she found? If she moved, she might scare it away.

Then Snarf pounced. He thrust his nose into a hollow in the ground among the heather. When he lifted it again a bird fluttered helplessly in his jaws. It was a ptarmigan. Snarf held it high, as though to ask, "Would you like some too?"

Hekja smiled and sat on the cold ground and watched while Snarf began his feast.

"Good dog," she said, and that was all.

* * *

So the days continued. Spring's flowers gave way to summer. The cows were growing fat.

Each morning Snarf left at dawn to hunt, returning with a fat belly and meat on his breath, and sometimes blood about his whiskers. He was a giant dog now.

But the girls still treated him as a runt, and Hekja as an interloper. Hekja was different—because of

Snarf, because Bran liked her, because she was poor. A girl without a dowry had no right to look at the chief's son. Maybe, thought Hekja, I'd be different anyway. Did any of the other girls ever gaze at the horizon, or dream of running with the wind?

It felt strange to be so lonely, with the other girls around her. She had never known it was possible to feel as alone as this. Even Banna avoided Hekja these days.

Now that there was lots of milk to work with, the other girls stayed together at the sheiling to make the butter and cheese. It was Hekja's job alone to run after the cows and stop them straying over the cliffs, and to bring them in for milking at the end of each day. Snarf nipped at their heels and barked when they didn't obey. Without him, it would have been more loneliness than she could bear.

Chapter 6

Danger on the Mountain

The dried bracken bed crunched under her as Hekja rolled over and tried to go back to sleep. It must still be a long way from dawn, she decided, for Snarf still lay beside her, with his comforting, furry warmth.

Just a few more days until Ma would be here with the other women, to take the cheese and butter back, and to bring them more rennet[8] and barley cake and cooked fish.

And for a while there'd be someone to talk to, to tell how Snarf had nearly caught an eagle, napping on a ledge, and how he'd learned to catch a dried cowpat in his teeth.

"Arf," said Snarf softly. His cold nose touched her cheek.

Hekja stroked him without opening her eyes. "Sshh. Go back to sleep," she whispered.

---

[8] The dried strips of calf stomach needed to turn the skimmed milk solid, so it could be chopped into tiny pieces and hung in cheesecloths from the sheiling rafters, to drain before the women took it back to press for cheese.

"Woof!" said Snarf more urgently. And then he whined.

Hekja opened her eyes.

All she could see was a world of white. The whiteness even swirled inside the doorway, cold and damp, the noises muffled as though the white had smothered them as well.

Hekja sat up, so the bracken bed crackled, and hugged Snarf close. "Fog," she said.

Snarf whined again. It was the first fog he had ever seen, Hekja realized. Even she had never seen a fog like this.

The other girls were stretching now, yawning and rubbing the sleep from their eyes. Reena peered out the door. "Ugh, I hate fog. The cows won't go far in this," she muttered.

"They'll still need milking, though," said Janna, looking nervously out into the fog.

Reena nodded at Hekja. "No need for us all to get cold and damp. You and the dog can bring the cows over here for the milking."

For a moment Hekja thought about refusing. But what was the point? And anyway, Snarf would need to go out, to have a drink. No matter how strange the white world was, she was sure Snarf could smell the way back to the sheiling.

"Here, boy," she said. But Snarf had already disappeared outside.

The whiteness closed about her as she followed

him. Behind her she heard Raina laughing. "With a bit of luck that stupid dog will fall over a cliff."

"Do all dogs stink?" asked Janna.

"Not proper dogs," declared Raina scornfully. "Our dogs never smell."

Of course they smell, thought Hekja. *Dogs always smell of dog.* She wondered what humans smelled like to dogs. *We girls probably smell of cheese*, she decided.

She stopped suddenly. Where was she? Even the sheiling had disappeared. Where was Snarf? And the cows?

"Arf," said Snarf happily, prancing up beside her, his tail pounding against her legs.

"Bring in the cows!" ordered Hekja. "Can you do that, boy? The cows!"

"Arf arf," said Snarf, as though to say, "Of course I can!" Snarf bounded off into the fog. Hekja grinned as she listened to him yipping at the cattle's heels, and the heavy beat of the cow's feet as they headed to the sheiling.

No one thanked her, or Snarf either, for bringing the cows in. Hekja sat with the others on their low wood stools, stroked a cow's teats, and listened to the milk as it squirt, squirt, squirted into the buckets. Every sound seemed muffled today, as though the fog was a cowhide blanket, covering everything. Even the birds were silent. How far did the fog stretch, wondered Hekja. All the way up to the sky? Was the whole world surrounded by fog, or just their mountain?

"It'll lift soon," said Reena confidently as the girls carried the milk buckets back into the sheiling and Hekja began to paddle yesterday's cream that had risen on the buckets overnight.

But the fog didn't lift. Hekja patted the last of the whey from the butter, while the other girls lay back on their beds and gossiped about who was the handsomest boy in the village, and who the strongest, and who had the best hand at the fishing nets.

Janna was sure that Bran was the handsomest. "And the strongest, too," she added, with a glance at Hekja. But Hekja ignored her.

Raina carefully avoided looking Hekja's way. "Ma says my brother's to marry the chief's daughter from Eagle Bay. She's got a grand dowry, Ma says."

Janna looked disappointed. "Maybe Bran won't want a stranger from Eagle Bay," she said hopefully.

Hekja gave the butter a harder pat than usual, and they all looked at her.

"Who do you fancy, Hekja?" asked Banna.

"No one," lied Hekja.

Reena laughed. "You must have your eye on someone! Of course, as a widow's daughter you can't hope for much. There's Jan Fisherman's son. You'd soon get used to his bandy legs."

"Or maybe you won't notice them in the dark,"

said Raina coarsely. They all laughed, except for Hekja.

Hekja refused to look up from the butter. "I'll think of that in a few years' time," she said as calmly as she could. "And not before."

Janna shrugged. "Well, there'll be no more boys in the village to choose from then than there are now."

"Unless the Vikings call!" giggled Raina.

The Vikings were the Norse raiders, who killed and stole and enslaved wherever they landed. But the Norsemen had never landed anywhere near the village. Vikings were after better booty than stone huts and cattle skins—they wanted gold from monasteries, walrus ivory or swords and armor from a king.

Janna giggled and poked Reena in the arm. "Just what you want for a husband! A Viking raider! At least he'd be big and strong!"

"Maybe a handsome stranger will be shipwrecked near our cove," said Banna dreamily. "We'll rescue him and he'll fall in love with one of us. . . ."

"With you, you mean. . . ." said Raina.

"He'll be a king's son with a palace and a golden throne, just like in the songs. . . ."

Reena laughed. "Who'd marry a stranger, even if he has a golden throne? Imagine living with people you don't know! Besides, you've never even met a stranger in your life."

"Yes, I have," said Banna. "The monk who came, years ago, remember?"

"You were only knee-high to a herring," objected Reena. "You can't remember back that far."

"Yes, I can," said Banna. "He had a squint. And he said that . . ."

Something bawled outside. It was a bellow of terror, then of pain. Snarf barked, then whined, and edged closer to Hekja.

"What is it?" cried Hekja.

Reena and Raina shrank back against the wall. "Wolf!" hissed Reena. "There's a wolf after the calves!"

"Everyone get back here!" ordered Raina. "A wolf won't come in here if we're alltogether!"

Hekja stared. "We can't let a wolf get the calves." She ran to the door, but Banna grabbed her arm.

"You can't go out there!" she cried. "Not with a wolf!"

"She's right!" Reena shook her head. "The wolf will only take a calf. If you go out there, it will kill you, too."

Hekja wrenched her arm free. "What if it's our calf! You have lots of calves, but Ma and I have only one!"

Hekja bit her lip and ran out into the fog. The world had disappeared. There was nothing but whiteness all around.

She tried to orient herself. The hut was . . . there. And the screaming came from . . . Hekja ran toward the noise.

The cows had scattered in terror, all but one. It was trying to butt the wolf with its long horns. And there in the whiteness was the long black shape of the wolf, circling around to snap at the calf again, but keeping well clear of the mother's horns.

Then suddenly the wolf stopped circling and sniffed toward Hekja instead. Hekja froze. She could almost hear its thought: here is an easier meal than a calf with a stroppy mother. Cows have horns, but girls don't.

What should she do? Helplessness washed over her. She had run out without thinking!

"Go away!" she yelled. Would sound alone frighten it? It was all she had. "Hoi hoi hoi!" she yelled. But the fog absorbed the noise. Even to her ears, her voice sounded thin and scared.

Suddenly the wolf vanished in the fog. But she knew it hadn't run away. The wolf was circling, trying to get behind her in the mist.

Suddenly something leaped behind her. Hekja screamed and swirled around, expecting the sharp jaws to close upon her. But it wasn't the wolf.

It was Snarf. He growled uncertainly deep within his throat. In the next instant he had leaped and had the wolf by the throat. He was smaller and less experienced, but Snarf had taken the wolf by surprise.

Hekja darted forward, then halted once again as the black shapes rolled and twisted in the fog.

The girls were screaming in the hut, but Hekja

didn't hear them until the rolling had stopped. Was it the wolf or Snarf who had won? She dared a step toward them. The wolf went limp, its teeth still grasping Snarf's leg. Then the great jaws fell open as the wolf rolled.

Snarf's first blow had ripped the wolf's windpipe. The enemy was dead.

Chapter 7

A Song for a Hero!

For a moment the two bodies lay on the grass, the fog sifting about them. Hekja dropped to her knees just as Snarf lifted his head, then struggled to his feet.

"What happened?" Banna raced from the sheiling and knelt beside her.

"I don't think he's hurt much," Kekja panted finally. "His ear is torn. But the wolf . . . the wolf . . ." Her voice choked.

"He's a hero," someone breathed. It was Reena. Hekja hadn't noticed the other girls come out of the sheiling.

"I've never known a dog fight a wolf all by itself," cried Raina.

"Come on," said Reena decisively. "Let's carry him inside. Janna, you get water to wash his wounds. Banna, we'll put him on your bed, it's warmest, and he can have my cloak. Hekja, do you think he'll eat barley bread, if we sop it first in cream?"

"Yes," said Hekja simply. Beside her, Snarf almost smiled.

* * *

Raina and Reena skinned the wolf carcass and hung it to dry over the rafters. The wolf skin would make a fine mat for Hekja's hearth at home. Snarf ate the wolf meat, and this time the girls didn't complain about the wolf stink on his breath.

That night Snarf slept by the door again, but this time it was a place of pride. Snarf was the guardian, the protector from the wolves. And Hekja was the Queen of the Mountain, because he was her dog.

It was hard to tell which one was the proudest.

Snarf drank his fill of milk every morning and evening after that, and the girls competed to scratch his ears or tickle his tummy. But Snarf was still Hekja's dog, and hers was the only voice that he obeyed.

He began to bring some of his catch home now, and basked in the praise. "Good dog!" they called, and, "Look what he's found now!"

"He's a better hunter than any of my father's dogs," Reena said, and Hekja agreed.

The girls plucked the feathers from the birds he caught to keep for bedding. They skinned the hares or squirrels and hung their skins up to dry for mats or blankets or clothes. But they left the meat for Snarf. There was no wood up on the mountain to cook anything, nor any dried peat turfs either, and it was too far for the women to cart turf up the hill. But Hekja gave her ma some of the meat when she came up with barley cakes and fish.

Until then Hekja had sung by herself, sometimes, as she and Snarf watched the cows. The song floated up along the cliffs until the eagles heard it, then drifted with the wind. But now she began to sing when the other girls could hear it.

This wasn't one of her father's songs, or one of the women's songs about grinding the barley, or bringing home the cows. This was a song that came to her with the wind, so it almost seemed she only had to open her mouth and the wind would sing the words for her.

> *"Mist on the hillside,*
> *Mist on the ground,*
> *The mist hid our cattle,*
> *And swallowed all sound*
>
> *"The wolf he came sneaking,*
> *But Snarfari he growled,*
> *He leaped at the wolf,*
> *In one fearsome bound.*
>
> *"And there lay the wolf,*
> *By the valiant hound,*
> *His ear torn and bloody,*
> *The bravest around."*

It was only as the song died away that she realized the girls were all staring at her.

"I've never heard that song before!" Janna cried.

"Of course not, stupid," said Reena. "It was about Snarf. How could anyone have made up a song about Snarf before!"

"Arf," said the valiant hound complacently. He was draped across Hekja's lap and full of pride, as though he had understood every word.

"You really made that up all by yourself?" Raina asked.

Hekja nodded.

"I've never met anyone who made up songs! Make up one about me!" Reena demanded. "And sing it when we go back home!"

"And one about me?" added Raina jealously.

"I'll try," said Hekja.

Every evening after that Hekja would sing a song she'd made up during the day. They were songs about the girls bringing the cattle in from the mountain or about the cheeses hanging from the rafters, or the chief's daughters paddling the butter. Sometimes the girls would repeat them too, though none had a voice as high and true as Hekja's.

At midsummer, the whole village trooped up the mountain for a feast, the men loaded with driftwood and burning faggots to light the fire, a whole bull calf to roast, drinking horns, and barrels of barley beer. The other dogs sniffed about, checking where Snarf had marked rocks and trees and walls, but he sat in the sheiling doorway and growled at them. This was his territory.

Hekja sang Snarf's song that night, and everybody cheered. She sat with Bran by the fire, and even if the chief didn't look pleased, he didn't object, for Hekja had sung a song about him, too. It was about the time he took his boat out to search for the boys from the far hut, who had gone missing during a storm, even though the waves were washing in the wind. He found them clinging to their upturned craft and nearly drowned, and brought them safely to shore.

Most people had almost forgotten the day their chief had been a hero. But now the chief would be remembered as long as Hekja's song was sung.

Sometimes it seemed to Hekja that summer could never end, it was so good.

Chapter 8

Raiders!

It was one of those late-summer days when sea and sky seemed to be as one, each as gray as the other, the rain gusting with the wind. Even from the sheiling, the girls could see the waves crash upon the shore and the whitecaps across the sea.

The cows hung around the sheiling, as they usually did when the weather was bad. It was the most sheltered spot on the mountain, which was why the hut had been built there. On some of the slopes, the wind could almost blow a cow away.

The girls lay on their bracken beds with Snarf flopped across Hekja and Banna—he was too big now for one lap alone—while Banna scratched his tummy and Hekja scratched behind his ears. Hekja gazed out at the rain as the wind lashed the walls and trickles of dirty water seeped through the roof. The women had been up the day before to take back the cheeses and the butter, so there was fresh barley cake to eat, and the chief's wife had even brought a giant stuffed fish head, boiled in their big iron pot.

The rain eased as the day wore on, but the wind still howled, as loud as Snarf when he decided he'd sing too. Reena and Raina shared out the fish head and gave Snarf the bones to chew, then Raina squelched out of the sheiling for a call of nature. But she had gone only a few steps when she flew back inside.

"Ships!" she yelled, her wet brown hair plastered to her face.

Her sister scrambled to her feet. "Where?"

"Out past the islands!" cried Raina.

None of the village boats should have been out in weather like this. The girls raced out the door and stared out to sea, their plaits blowing in the wind and their dresses flattened against their bodies. "Look!" ordered Raina.

Hekja stared at the gray ocean. Yes, there were ships out there, like no ships that she had ever seen. The village boats were round with a short, stubby sail. These ships were long, with giant sails, and crowded with people. One even had a horse on board. They were making straight for the village harbor.

"Vikings!" whispered Hekja.

"How do you know?" asked Janna tremulously. "You've never seen a Viking ship!"

"Who else would they be?" demanded Hekja impatiently. "None of the island boats are as big as that!"

"But why would Vikings come here?" whispered

Banna. It was as though she was trying to convince herself it wasn't true. "There's nothing here to steal."

"The storm must have blown them off course! Come on! We have to warn the village! They won't have seen them yet!"

"No!" Reena's voice held real terror. "We can't go down there!"

"We have to!"

"You fool! You know what Vikings do to people!"

"That's why we have to warn the village!" cried Hekja, suddenly sounding like a chief's daughter.

"Think!" Reena yelled. "By the time we got there, the Vikings would have landed. At least we're safe up here. Better that some of our village survives than none at all!"

"So we should wait up here in safety and let the village die?" cried Hekja.

"Better that than kill us all! And here we have the cows and shelter!"

"No! We have to try!" Hekja looked around wildly. And with that she was flying down the mountain, her face against the wind.

"Hekja!" cried Reena.

But Hekja had gone, with Snarf bounding after her.

Chapter 9

Attack!

The path twisted and turned as Hekja ran down the great mountain. Soon she could no longer see the ships, just hills and the gray distance of the sky and sea. Behind her Snarf leaped and pranced, as though he was sure it was a game.

The path curved past the witch's hut near the stream. The witch stared as Hekja ran past.

Hekja didn't even pause. "Viking ships!" she yelled.

"Girl! Come back here!" shouted Tikka, but her words were swallowed by the wind. Hekja had gone.

Finally the path curved again. The village was below them. Hekja stopped, and stared, and tried to still her breath. Beside her Snarf flopped down onto his tummy and whined at the smell of blood.

Reena had been right, Hekja realized. She was too late. No one could help the village now.

Big men, taller than she had ever thought a man could be, with bright hair that streamed out beneath metal helmets. Bright eyes, in bearded faces, and bright swords, too. They strode above the bodies of the villagers. Why do dead people look so small, thought Hekja numbly.

The stench of death was everywhere, a strong, sweet smell, overpowering even the smells of fish and salt.

Snarf whimpered again. He had killed a wolf and hunted game. But even to him, this smell seemed wrong.

Someone screamed, far away. Hekja could hear sobbing, too, and a faint clang, clanging that she had never heard before.

Her mind fought free of shock. She had to get to Ma! Hekja glanced around, then made for the shelter of a byre. She signaled to Snarf to follow her. He needed no urging, and clung close to her heels.

They slipped from wall to wall, from one hut to the next. They passed by the chief's hut now and saw the chief's wife, lying sprawled upon the stones. Snarf's mother must have tried to defend her mistress, for there was a great cut across her neck.

Hekja knelt by the chief's wife and cradled her head in her lap. The woman blinked at her, as though it was hard to see. "No!" she whispered. "Don't stay here, child. Run!"

"Ma?" whispered Hekja.

The chief's wife groaned and shook her head. "Get away. Go!"

Snarf whined and bent to lick the woman's face.

Hekja laid her hand on his head and whispered, "Quiet." Her hand was steady, even though her voice was not. She laid the chief's wife back gently on the stones and crept back to the shelter of the wall.

They kept on going.

There was another body, Banna's ma, bloody and white. She was still breathing, although she didn't move. Another body, not far away—the chief—his body wet with blood. His empty eyes stared at the sea. Three of his men lay about him. They were dead. They had to be dead. No man could live with wounds like that.

Hekja kept her hand on Snarf, to warn him to be quiet. But he didn't need her warning now.

The clanging sounds were coming from the other side of the hut. Hekja peered around the corner.

"Bran," she whispered. But there was too much noise for Bran to hear her.

Bran held a sword awkwardly in both his hands. It wasn't his—there was no sword in the whole village, just knives and the chief's big axe. Bran must have grabbed it from one of the Vikings.

A Viking stood before him, and they banged their swords together. But even to Hekja it was clear that the Viking was playing with the youth, letting him try to hit while the Viking weaved aside and laughed.

Then all at once the Viking seemed to lose his patience. He struck a blow at Bran's head that sent him down.

Hekja's pa had sung a song once about a warrior who died gazing in his loved one's eyes. But there was no way for Hekja to reach Bran now. He simply lay there at the viking's feet, his blood spilling on the ground. Hekja gripped Snarf's fur so hard that her fingers hurt. But still she made no sound, and neither did the dog.

There was nothing she could do for Bran.

They crept along the wall, Hekja first and Snarf following, reluctant. Another woman's body, and another. They were nearly at Hekja's hut now, and suddenly before them there was Hekja's mother, sprawled on her back on the shingle stones, with two men standing over her.

Hekja stared, but the scene wavered in front of her, as though water had washed over it. It was impossible . . . impossible. How could one person do that to another? Her skin prickled with the horror. Then suddenly her vision cleared, and she ran forward.

Hekja's ma was white with terror and twisted with pain, too. But she saw Hekja and she screamed out, "Run!"

That was the last thing she ever said. One of the men—the largest one Hekja had seen, with a chin like a cod fish and almost no beard at all—plunged his sword into her mother's heart, then pulled it out, all bloody.

Hekja screamed. It was a scream that held all the horror of Bran's death, the devastation of her village, all her grief and pain. She ran toward her ma's body and knelt down. Her ma's eyes stared at the sky, and there was a froth of blood from her mouth.

The beardless man grabbed Hekja's arm and hauled her up to her feet. He grinned. His teeth were as white as a wolf's.

"This one is mine!" he roared. The words sounded strange to Hekja, but his meaning was plain.

The other man laughed. He had blood upon his hands and on his face and elsewhere, too, but he could still laugh. "You've had your share, Finnbogi!" he cried. He pulled Hekja away. She stumbled against his body and half fell.

"No such thing!" the man called Finnbogi cried. For a moment the men glared, as though they were about to fight each other.

Hekja struggled, kicking and trying to bite. The man just laughed, then screamed. Snarf had leaped at him, silent as a spear, and bitten him behind the knee so deeply that his teeth met through the tendons.

The man dropped Hekja. He turned and grabbed at Snarf, but Snarf was leaping across the shingle. Hekja raced after him, sobbing, her face smeared with tears and her ma's blood.

Snarf slowed down to let her catch up to him. Behind them the first man was examining his leg. But the man called Finnbogi galloped after them.

"What the—?" A woman stepped out of the chief's hut. She was a Viking, the first Viking woman Hekja had seen. She wore a dress, finer than any the village women wore, and a caplike helmet like the men, with bright red hair beneath it. In her arms she held the chief's best ale horns, carved and inlaid with bronze. They were the only good things in the hut, passed down from chief to chief. But the village had no chief now.

"Get her, Finnbogi!" the woman called to the man, as though delighted by the chase.

Hekja swerved. She raced past the chief's hut, then along the track that led to the sheiling. Then suddenly she veered. That path led to the girls. She couldn't lead the Vikings there!

Finnbogi was winded already. He carried his heavy sword and shield, and he hadn't spent the summer racing after cows on mountain slopes like Hekja had. She could hear him gasping, but there was no time to turn to see how close he was. They ran through the cow field, past the chief's bull, then over the stone fence. The man then leaned against the fence, panting.

Hekja risked a glance. He'd given up!

Then someone yelled behind her, "You're past it, Finnbogi! Leave it to those with proper beards!"

Another called, "Let me show you how it's done, Finnbogi!"

Finnbogi growled. "You see if you can catch her, Leif. She must have feet like falcon's wings!"

Suddenly another man's footsteps joined the chase.

"Go to it, Leif!" It was the Viking woman, her voice high and clear above the men's.

They fled down to the beach and along the shingle. Leif's leather shoes slipped on the wet rocks but Hekja's and Snarf's feet were sure. Around the bay, and up the other side. It seemed to Hekja as though the world had narrowed to her feet pounding on the pebbles, breath tearing at her lungs, and the speedy beat of Snarf's feet at her heels. The cliff reared up before them, with its path of dirt and stones.

The man was gaining now, as he was new to the chase and they were not. Even Snarf was panting, and Hekja's breath seemed torn from deep within her body. It was impossible to go any faster up the path— any misstep might mean she slid back down, into the waiting arms of the Viking, who was nearly on them. His sword flashed down, just behind Snarf's tail. At the cliff's top, Hekja tried to think. Which way now? There was one path that might lead them to safety, if only she could make it. It was a hunter's path from the village, up into the hills. If she and Snarf could get up there, they'd be safe, hidden among the cliffs and mountain crags.

Hope gave her strength. Her feet pounded along the path, sure-footed as a hare. Suddenly something slashed across her ankles. Hekja fell forward, wanting to scream, but there was only enough breath for a gasp of horror and despair.

Hekja tried to rise. A hard foot held her down.

Strong, small hands grasped her wrists and tied them roughly.

Hekja struggled to see who held her. Was it the man, Finnbogi, who had killed her mother? Would she suffer the same fate? But when Hekja turned, it was a woman's face—the woman she had seen before. One hand held Hekja's hair, close to her scalp, to stop her from trying to run. The other held a sword. It was this that Hekja had stumbled over, held out flat to trip her as she ran.

Leif was on them now. He leaned over, trying to catch his breath, then looked up and grinned. "So you have caught my fish for me, little sister," he panted to the woman. He sounded his words strangely, but they were familiar enough for Hekja to understand.

The woman laughed and let the sword dangle by her skirts. She was young, her hair the same bright color as the man's. There were rings on her fingers, a gold band on her arm, brooches on her dress, and a necklace, too, with almost enough metal to make a cooking pot.

"You're getting soft, Leif. Too much time sitting on your bum on board the ship. Your legs have forgotten what they're for."

Leif hauled Hekja up roughly by her hair. "She's mine now, at any rate."

"She's not," said the woman cooly. "I was the one who caught her. I claim her."

Hekja gazed frantically from one to the other, trying to follow their speech. How could she escape? And where was Snarf? Please, she thought, please, Snarf, go to Tikka or the girls. You'll be safe there. Go, or the Vikings will get you too.

Leif stared at the woman. "Are you serious, Freydis? What do you want with another thrall?" He looked at Hekja contemptuously. "She'll be quite unskilled coming from a poor place like this."

The woman, Freydis, laughed again. "Did you see how fast she ran? She's a runner, Leif. Faster than your man Hikki."

"No one is faster than Hikki," said Leif, amused. "He was a present from the king himself."

Freydis shrugged. "We will see," she said calmly. "Will you take the girl to my ship, dear brother, or will I?"

For a moment it looked like Leif would argue. Then he dropped Hekja suddenly, so she landed back on the wet ground. "Take her," he said abruptly, and walked off, down to the shore.

"Please," began Hekja. Surely a woman would be kinder than a man. "Please let me go. . . ."

There was a growl behind them. Snarf leaped, as he had leaped at the man Finnbogi and the wolf. His jaws met where the woman's knees would be, underneath her skirts.

But the cloth got in the way. Snarf reared back, to strike again. But the woman was swifter. She lifted her sword and struck him hard against his neck.

The dog collapsed.

"No," whispered Hekja. "No."

The woman glanced at her. "He was trying to protect you, wasn't he? That dog has courage." She gestured to one of the passing men. "Carry him to my ship." She looked around the village contemptuously. "He's worth more than anything else in this place."

"He's . . . not dead?" stammered Hekja.

The woman looked amused. "I used the flat of my sword on him, not the blade. Now, will you walk, or must you be carried too?"

Hekja tried to understand. But the accent was so strong. Her mind was numb with pain and exhaustion. But the word "walk" at least was clear.

"I'll walk," said Hekja.

* * *

The big ships bounced on the waves far out in the harbor, but there were smaller boats pulled up on the pebbles in the bay. One of the men shoved Hekja roughly into the nearest one. It was already piled with bags of barley, and the iron pot that Hekja recognized as the chief's.

It took two men to carry Snarf. They flung him into the bottom of the boat, then pushed it out into the waves.

Hekja knelt by Snarf. She wanted to hold his head in her lap, or stroke him, but her hands were bound tight. She gazed about her. Ships, so many ships, and the shore growing more distant. Tears stung her eyes. She looked down at Snarf instead. Was he moving?

Suddenly his eyes opened. He blinked and tried to get up.

"Shh. Don't move." She was afraid that if he tried to jump out, they'd hit him again. "Stay, boy. Stay."

Snarf whined. He tried to sit up, then collapsed down again. The tears were blinding her now, but it didn't matter. There was nothing she wanted to see. Hekja laid her face on Snarf's fur as the boat bobbed out toward the waiting ships.

Back on shore where the Vikings would sleep, driftwood fires lit the darkness . Hekja had never smelled wood fires before—wood was far too precious to burn. They sparked higher than any fire she'd ever seen, like tiny stars reaching for the sky.

Chapter 10

The Ship

It was dawn when she opened her eyes again. Snarf still slept, but his breathing was even. Hekja looked around. Ships, lots of ships, each one far longer than even the chief's hut and as wide.[9]

The ships smelled of pine trees. Each had a giant square sail of dripping woolen cloth across the middle that the men raised to catch the wind. There were two platforms either end, with bundles stowed underneath, and a deep middle bit, which was where Hekja sat with Snarf amid even more bundles. Oars dangled from the rowlocks at either end.

Gulls screamed above them in the growing light, and the clouds skidded across the sky. All around the Vikings were heading back to their ships, folding their tents on shore and splashing through the

[9] These ships were of the kind known as knarr, or knorr, though that term may not have referred to a cargo ship until a century or so later; they were wider and deeper than a longship. Longships, or drekars, were longer and faster, with oars all the way along each side, and were used for raiding along the coast of northern Europe; knarrs were used on long voyages across the Atlantic Ocean.

shallows, their arms full of whatever they had stolen—cooking pots and cheeses, calf skins and dried fish. Someone had even put a ramp down into the shallows from one of the ships and was leading the chief's bull through the waves.

The poor beast looked terrified and tried to bolt, till the man gave it a whack about the rear with the blunt of his sword.

Hekja knew how the bull was feeling. Where had her life gone, the only life she'd known? Where were the villagers? Were they all dead, except the girls up on the great mountain and the witch?

Hekja looked up the hill, but no smoke hovered up above the witch's fire. Either she had the sense to put it out, or else they had killed her, too.

She spotted Finnbogi, who had killed her ma. He still had the blood on his shirt, but he didn't even glance at Hekja as he passed. She was just one more piece of loot.

No one seemed concerned with her at all. They were busy setting sail, stacking goods, and settling themselves comfortably against the bundles.

Freydis was the only woman on board, standing amidships and directing men to stow this here and stow that there. A tall, short-bearded man Hekja hadn't seen before stood by her side, bellowing orders.

Hekja looked on wide-eyed. As the ships began to wallow out from the calm of the bay and plunge into the wild ocean waves. What was happening?

Where were they going now?

She should have known they wouldn't stay there, but she hadn't thought of where they might be headed. Hekja had lived her life by the sea, but this was the first time she had been on it. She stared at the distant shore as the village grew farther and farther away. Then suddenly she saw a figure striding out onto the cliff top above the waves, her cloak wrapped tight about her.

It was the witch. As Hekja watched, she lifted her arm and waved. How much had Tikka guessed, when she named a fat little puppy Riki Snarfari, thought Hekja. How far are we going to travel now?

Chapter 11

Under Sail

Now there were only gray waves and the gray sky above. Freydis strode across to Hekja. Even on the swaying ship her walk was confident, as though she had been born on one. She carried a dipper of fresh water, and some dried fish dangled from her hand. She held the dipper up to Hekja's mouth and let her drink deeply, and then she let Snarf drink as well.

"Well?" she demanded, staring down at Hekja. Even the Viking women, Hekja thought, were taller than a village man. "If I untie you, will you scream and jump overboard? It's too far to swim to shore, you know, even if you can swim, which I doubt."

Hekja said nothing. Some of Freydis's words were strange, so she was not sure what they meant.

Freydis laughed. It seemed she liked laughing, though not everyone might like the things she chose to laugh at. "Hikki!" she called. "Come here!"

"Yes, mistress?"

A young man, with dark hair and eyes, made his

way uncertainly across the boat. His face looked slightly green. He was taller than any village man, even Bran, though he was not as tall as even the shortest of the Vikings.

He glanced at Hekja curiously, then saw the dried fish in Freydis's hands. He dashed to the side and vomited into the sea.

Freydis laughed even louder. "Stop feeding the fish, Hikki!" she shouted. "I ordered you to come over here!"

The man wiped his mouth and staggered back. Freydis pointed to Hekja. "You're from her land originally, are you not?" she demanded.

"Yes, mistress, though I have lived in Norway for many years."

"And now you no longer live in Norway. You are my brother's thrall, on my ship, and you will do what I say. Untie her, explain things to her, get her to eat. Teach her our language."

Hikki stared. "She should understand you already, mistress!"

Freydis shrugged. "These tiny villages on these islands only use half a dozen words. She probably doesn't know a loom from a codfish. Tell her what she needs to know."

"That will take some time, mistress!"

"Then the sooner you begin, the better," said Freydis without much interest. "Feed her too!" She thrust the dried fish into Hikki's unwilling hands, then strode

59

back to the front of the ship and sat staring at the sea, as though she could understand its waves.

Hikki put the fish down and untied the rope from Hekja's hands. The rope was wet and the knots hard to undo, but finally he managed it. Hekja gave a small groan as the blood flowed back into her hands and feet, then bit her lip. She wouldn't give the Vikings the pleasure of hearing her pain. But none of them were listening; they were chattering to themselves, or pulling ropes about the sail.

"Who are you?" demanded Hekja softly as Snarf sniffed the young man's feet, rejected them, and took a fish to chew instead.

"I am Hikki, runner for King Harald the Fair Hair,"[10] said the young man proudly. "Now a gift to Leif Eriksson, the son of the great chief Erik the Red, the founder of Greenland. Leif brought many goods to trade with Norway, and Erik the Red sent his son to the king with gifts of walrus ivory and furs. The king gave me to Leif in return. I am the fastest runner in the whole of Norway. I took messages from one end of the land to the other."

"Norway? Greenland? What are these names?" asked Hekja, bewildered.

"They are countries, far from your village. Norway is where this ship has sailed from," said Hikki patiently. "Greenland is where we are going. It's a new land, found only eighteen years ago. My master

_____

[10] King Harald wasn't yet called the Fair Hair, but this is the name he would be known by.

and your mistress have holdings there, near their father's farm at Brattahlid. The Lady Freydis is your mistress now. She is my master's sister."

"We are going to another land?" Hekja had to force her voice to stay steady.

Hikki nodded. "The Norsemen know how to sail far across the sea and find their way even when there is no land to guide them. From Stad in Norway, it is seven days" sailing to eastern Iceland, then four days' sailing to Brattahlid in Greenland."

Hekja blinked. It was too much to understand.

"We were sailing to Brattahlid, but the storm blew us off course," Hikki continued. "The Vikings had to shelter in your bay, so my master says now we will sail well to the south of Iceland and, God willing,[11] see land in eight days' time."

Hekja shook her head. "Eight? Seven?"

Hikki sighed. "They are numbers, for counting. You have a lot to learn." He held up his fingers. "You see—one, two, three, four, five. Ten are the fingers of two hands. But there are bigger numbers. Erik the Red took four hundred followers with him to Greenland. That is a larger number by far."

Hikki patted Hekja's hand, till she drew it back. "I was as ignorant as you are when I was taken as a boy," he added.

Hekja stared at him. "The Vikings captured you, too?"

---

[11] By 999, when this story is set, most Norse people were Christian.

Hikki nodded. "I am a slave, a thrall like you."

"A slave! Why didn't you run away then," Hekja demanded, "when they landed at my village? You said you are the best runner in . . . in wherever it is!"

Hikki looked superior. "And live among the rocks and hares? Greenland is an empty land, my master says. If I serve him well, I will be freed and may claim land of my own,[12] and have a proper farm, not a hut with a scraping of barley behind it. Even . . ."—he looked calculatingly at Hekja—"a wife."

Hekja ran her hands across Snarf's ears. They at least were familiar and comforting. "So I am a slave," she said slowly. "What does a slave do?"

"What her mistress tells her to do. What did you do back in your village?"

Hekja shrugged. "I herded the cows, paddled the butter, made the cheese, dug the turfs . . . what everybody does."

"Then doubtless you will make cheese in Greenland. It sounds a fine, green place," said Hikki enthusiastically. "There must be mountains of grass all year round, to have a name like that."

"And the father of your master and my mistress, you said he is a chief there?"

Hikki nodded. "His name is Erik. They call him Erik the Red. A great man, by all accounts. A hero.

---

[12] Vikings were great traders, and thralls were one of the most commonly traded items, captured in all the countries where Vikings fought. Thralls could be freed by their owners, in return for special service, or their freedom could be bought by others.

My master Leif Eriksson is a hero, too," he added proudly. "Leif made a voyage to yet another new land, Vinland, just last year. That is where he traded for the fine furs he took to Norway this summer, to trade for other things."

"What things?" asked Hekja. She picked up one of the dried fish and began to pull it apart, nibbling some of it and feeding the rest to Snarf with her fingers.

"Flour for bread and malt for beer, iron, linen, wax and tin, weapons, cooking pots, glass beads for the women, a good horse to ride and one to pull the plough. Many things," said Hikki. He looked at Snarf, as the big dog chewed the second fish. "That is a fine hound," he added.

"He is mine," said Hekja proudly.

Hikki shook his head. "You are a thrall, a slave. He is Freydis's dog now." He gave a shrug. "A good dog like him is worth more than a thrall, though not as much as a runner like me."

"He is mine!" flared Hekja.

Hikki looked at her consideringly. "You will learn," he said at last. "Now you must study the Norse words, as your mistress ordered."

For a moment Hekja wanted to argue. She didn't want to learn the strange new words. She didn't want Hikki's company either.

But at least he wasn't a Viking. And perhaps he could tell her something that might be useful so that somehow . . . somehow, she could get away.

Chapter 12

Storm

The day dragged on. Hikki droned more words. Some she knew, and some she didn't, but she repeated them anyway, just to pass the time. The wind lashed at the boat, and the salt spray splattered them. Snarf's napping area at the bottom of the boat slowly became a puddle.

There was no land, though Hekja searched the skyline. The world was featureless, gray, and gray and more gray. How could the Vikings know which way to go in a world like this? Maybe, thought Hekja, they would sail forever, and the world would never change. She was too numb now even to care.

Someone handed Hekja a dipper and told her to bail out the water. The ship was heavy loaded, and already rode low among the waves. Hekja dipped, and threw, and dipped again. Snarf rested his face on her lap as though to say, "I'd help you if I could."

There was dried fish to eat that night. Hekja had eaten dried fish all her life, either smoked by the fire or just hung in the wind outdoors till it was too hard and dry to rot, but in the village dried fish was soaked in milk or water to soften it. Here on the ship the fish were so hard, you had to gnaw at them. Hekja shredded some of hers and took the bones out for Snarf to eat. Some of the Vikings also ate long strips of hard dried meat. But they didn't offer it to Hekja, or Hikki.

I am a slave, she thought. I am a slave. The words kept pounding through her. She knew what slaves were, but had never really thought about it before. No matter what I do, how well I make the butter or how well I guard the cows, I will be worthless, a slave.

She and Snarf slept among the bundles. The Vikings had sleeping bags with fur inside, but no one offered Hekja any covering at all. It was dawn when she woke, the sun a red gleam on the horizon. It rose slowly in the sky till it hung high above the ship. Even through the clouds, it seemed hotter than the sun over the great mountain. And there was no shade. The sail flapped and people yelled and the sea lashed over the side.

The sun sank again. The Vikings crawled into their sleeping bags once more, two to each sack, except the men who watched the sail. Even Hikki had a cloak to wrap himself in. Hekja held Snarf to her.

Then a voice came from the darkness. "Here."

It was Freydis. She threw a couple of rough, cured cowskins down to Hekja and made her way unerringly through the bundles, back to her sleeping bag and husband at the front of the boat.

The skins smelled like home. Hekja wrapped one about her shoulders and the other about her legs and Snarf, and they curled up together in the damp of the ship.

* * *

Three more days passed, each one like the one before. Only the colors changed, a sea and sky of gray or green or blue. The swaying ship didn't seem so strange now. Hekja knew its smells and movements. She even knew how to relieve herself over the swaying rail, though unlike the Vikings, she waited for darkness.

Sometimes the other ships sailed close enough for the Vikings to yell at each other across the sea, cheery insults that Hekja couldn't understand. But mostly each ship was a floating world of its own.

Suddenly Freydis's husband, Thorvard, gave a yell and pointed high up in the sky.

Hekja followed his gaze. It was a bird.

Someone cheered and clapped Thorvard on the back. Freydis strode down from her spot on the prow, and they began to confer, gazing at the sky and sea.

Hekja looked back at Hikki. "What is all the fuss? It's just a bird."

"It's a land bird," said Hikki, looking superior. "It means that we are close to land."

"Greenland?"

Hikki shook his head. "Iceland."

Hekja shivered. The name sounded cold and strange. "Are we going to land there? Would they kill more people like the Vikings did back home?"

"Of course not!" Hikki looked scornful. "The Greenlanders came from Iceland. Remember? I told you so! No, we won't land on Iceland. The cargo boats are full already. We shall keep sailing to Brattahlid."

Hekja nodded. What did it matter? If there were Vikings in Iceland she couldn't escape there. But Greenland . . . it sounded different. Hikki had said it was an empty land. There would be places for her and Snarf to hide . . . and then . . . Hekja bit her lip. What then?

* * *

Snarf smelled it first. He lifted his nose and whined.

"What is it?" Hekja bent toward him. Snarf whined again.

Now the Vikings seemed to sense it too. Thorvard yelled an order and waved his arm at the sail. It was sagging now the wind had dropped. Freydis strode about the ship, gesturing to the store piles. Men began to tighten ropes.

"I said pull in the sail!" bellowed Thorvard. "Are none of you fools listening to me?"

"What is it?" cried Hekja.

Hikki shook his head. He mostly sat with Hekja these days. Hekja supposed it made him feel important, having someone who knew less than him. Suddenly the sail flopped down behind them. The ship stopped its onward pace and rolled a little in the waves.

Hekja gazed around. "Why are we stopping? There is no land here!"

One of the Vikings heard her. He grinned. "Storm coming!"

Thorvard clambered to the rear of the boat and hailed the ship behind.

"Leif!" he shouted. "What do you think? A bad one?"

The ship behind came closer. "Better lighten the ship!" yelled Leif. He grinned. "You can throw my sister overboard for a start!"

"I heard that, brother mine!" Freydis shouted at him. "Lighten your own ship, if you want. This ship has sailors on it, not sit-at-homes, frightened of a tiny wind!"

"This storm will have even more breath than you!" yelled Leif cheerfully. "See you at home, dear sister! I'll bet you a nice new shawl we beat you back!"

"Keep your shawls to warm your feet!" shouted Freydis.

Leif grinned in return, then turned and bellowed orders to his crew.

The first gust hit. The ship lurched wildly, one side dipping deep into the water, so the waves sloshed in. Hikki yelled, then grabbed the side.

The next gust was even stronger. Then the wind bit, and didn't let them go.

Hekja had thought the boat shuddered before. Now it lashed from side to side. Snarf whined and crawled into the middle of the ship. Hekja followed. She grabbed one of the struts and held it with one hand, her knuckles white. The other arm stretched around Snarf. The rain came like a curtain, each drop so cold and sharp that it bit into her skin. It was impossible to see across the ship.

Up, up, up . . . Hekja had thought the sea was flat, but the ship seemed to climb a great mountain. Then down the other side, the wave crashing white around them. The ship shuddered further down into the trough, then up again.

It was like mountains had risen all across the sea.

Someone screeched in Hekja's ear. "Bail!"

Hekja nodded. She held Snarf by the scruff of the neck in one hand and used a water jar to scoop out the icy water with the other. It seemed they were only inches from the sea.

The ship lurched down again. A giant wave crashed behind them. Its foam lashed across the ship, carrying Snarf with it. The big dog tried frantically to paddle. Hekja caught one glimpse of his terrified face, then he was gone.

"No!" Hekja dived after him, reaching through the foam. Yes . . . yes . . . her fingers touched his fur before the water closed over her and spat her out over the rail of the ship.

Almost instinctively she kept hold of Snarf's fur as

they went under. Was this what it was like to drown? Had her brothers felt this cold confusion before they died? Snarf was so limp. She wouldn't let him die! Hekja pushed downward with her free arm and legs, forcing her body upward, so it dragged Snarf up too. Was he still alive, wondered Hekja desperately.

Then something hauled her up. No, not up. Up had no meaning. Something dragged her through the water and dropped her on the heaving deck. A moment later, Snarf landed, sprawling on top of her.

"A mermaid!" Freydis cried. She was laughing still. "And a hairy fish!" Hekja reached for Snarf, just as he coughed and tried to struggle to his feet. Hekja grabbed him again, but her hands felt cold and weak.

"Thorvard!" yelled Freydis. "We need rope! Bring it here!"

Thorvard clambered across the ship. Even in this weather his step was firm, as though his body moved with the ship. "Tie the girl to the mast, and the dog as well," Freydis shouted.

"The dog?"

"I didn't fish him out to lose him overboard again!" yelled Freydis.

Thorvard grinned. His beard was flecked with foam. He grabbed Snarf by the scruff of the neck and dragged him over to the mast. Snarf whined and tried to get away. But at least, thought Hekja, he was still alive.

She tried to stand, then crawled instead through

the water at the bottom of the ship, till she reached the mast too. It was a relief to feel the rope about her waist, tying her securely. Snarf was already tied about his neck and chest.

"Bail!" Thorvard yelled, forcing a bucket into Hekja's limp hands.

Hekja bailed. Her throat hurt, her body ached. It even hurt to breathe. But if bailing helped them survive, then she'd keep on going. Half the time it seemed the waves just lashed the water back. But at least a little reached over the rail.

Hekja could see Thorvard at the rudder, forcing the ship through the storm. Even Freydis worked with the rowers now, heaving the great oars back and forth to give the ship what little power they could to ride the waves.

No, it would never end, thought Hekja. But slowly the wind died down, and the rain stopped. The seas stayed as high as ever.

The waves crashed around them all that night, and no one slept. Black sky, black air, black sea. Only the frothing wave tops showed any white at all. But with the first gray light of dawn, it was clear the worst was over.

When Hekja woke, she was still hanging limply from the rope, and the sea was calm. Men were yelling, trying to find the ships that had accompanied them before. But there was no answer except the lap of waves, and everything was white.

Chapter 13

The Iceberg

"Arf," Snarf barked beside her, as though there was a monster in the fog that only he could see.

Then someone screamed out, "Berg!"

Something loomed beside them, tall as a hill and gleaming, even though there was no sun to light it. The men scrambled to their rowlocks and heaved with their whole bodies at the oars.[13]

It was as though the something breathed out cold and made the hair on Hekja's neck rise.

"What's happening?" she cried.

Hikki clung onto the side of the ship and shook his head. Terror had stopped his tongue. His face was almost as white as the fog. "It is the end of the world," he muttered through chattering teeth.

Freydis glanced at them, then strode across the ship. She lifted Hekja's chin with her fingers. "You were brave enough last night," she commented. "I like that. Let's see how brave you are today."

---

[13] They would have stood to row, not sat as rowers do today.

"What is it?" cried Hekja, gesturing toward the monster in the sea.

"Just an iceberg," said Freydis. "It wants to crush us. We shall see who wins." She glanced back at the iceberg as though amused at its challenge.

Suddenly Snarf barked again. It was a sharp sound in the cold air. He pointed with his nose, as he might do at a hare or deer. "Arf! Arf!"

Freydis glanced carelessly in the direction his nose pointed. Then suddenly she caught her breath as a new iceberg drifted into view. "Thorvard!" she yelled. "To port! To port!"

Thorvard heaved against the rudder. The ship veered. The iceberg passed, so close that if anyone had reached out of the ship, they might have touched it. Hekja heard a faint scraping underneath the water, where the ice grazed the ship a bit too close.

The ship lurched. But at least it held.

Even Freydis held her breath at that. She let it out again and its steam added to the fog. "Well," she said. She looked at Snarf with new interest. "Do you think he can smell an iceberg?"

Hekja shook her head. "We have never seen an iceberg before. He is a good hunter, though."

"But can he hunt icebergs too?" Freydis seemed to make up her mind without waiting for an answer. "Come," she said to Hekja. "The dog talks to you, I think. There is no time to teach him to talk to me.

Where there are two icebergs, there are more, and any one might kill us."

She strode back to the mast and untied Snarf. Snarf tried to stand, but his legs collapsed beneath him.

Hekja bent and picked him up. He was as long as she was now, so she had to haul his front, while his back legs trailed behind.

Hekja half carried, half dragged him to the prow of the ship. Snarf struggled to get down, but again his back legs collapsed beneath him, so he sat on his haunches, with as much dignity as he could, and stared out at the fog.

Nothing happened. Freydis shrugged. "It was just coincidence," she said. "I've never heard of a dog who—"

"Arf!" Snarf interrupted her. He pointed again, to the left this time. "Arf arf arf!"

"Far to starboard!" yelled Freydis. Another great white shape floated through the fog, though at least this was far enough away not to disturb the ship. She grinned at Hekja. "It seems it was worth saving him from the sea! A dog who can smell icebergs!"

The others in the boat were staring at them now. Snarf yipped, as though this was a great new game, and sniffed deep into the fog. Each time he sensed a new one, Snarf warned Thorvard at the helm so he was able to steer away in time.

"Arf!" Snarf barked, and "Arf arf arf!"

Iceberg after iceberg floated by. They were more blue than white, thought Hekja wonderingly, as though each had trapped a little of the sky. Perhaps that was where the sky had gone—it had been swallowed by the icebergs, leaving only the mist to take its place.

"Any sign of the other ships?" Freydis spoke quietly to her husband.

He shook his head. "Either we have drifted too far apart, or they were lost in the storm."

Freydis nodded. Even she did not laugh at that.

Chapter 14

Out from the Fog

When Hekja woke the next morning, she found someone had covered her with a sealskin rug, a proper sleeping sack that kept off the salt spray, unlike the cowhide blankets Freydis had given her before. The worst was behind them.

Snarf was a hero. This was a ship of heroes, Hekja thought, who faced storms and endless oceans and beat them both.

"I will call him Ice Nose," announced Freydis as she handed Hekja their breakfast.

Hekja shook her head. "His name is Riki Snarfari," she said firmly, meeting Freydis's gaze.

"His name is Ice Nose," said Freydis. Her eyes were as cool as an iceberg, and as blue. "He can be my dog, or he can be fish food. You choose."

Hekja gasped. Was this how she rewarded them? Then she remembered the village, how Freydis had laughed even with the smell of blood sharp in the salt air.

Hekja bowed her head. "He is your dog," she said. "His name is Ice Nose."

"Good," said Freydis. "I said you'd learn." She smiled. "I'll tell Leif you were worth saving, if the storm did not swallow him and his ship." She strode back to talk to her husband and the rowers.

Snarf sat his bottom on Hekja's feet, and she shared the food with him. It was better than they'd had before—dried beef as well as fish, though the beef was as tough as a bone. Hekja's face was wet, but she refused to wipe her eyes, lest others notice she was crying.

Despite their bravery in the storm, they were killers. And Freydis was just as bad.

But things changed after the storm. Before it had been as though Hekja and Snarf were simply cargo, like bales of cloth or barrels. Now at least the crew nodded as they passed.

And then one morning, as Hekja crossed the ship to throw one of Snarf's droppings overboard (a sailor had kicked him on the first day, when he had trodden in one), Freydis beckoned her to sit up by the prow.

Hekja settled herself on the damp boards, with Snarf at her feet. At first Freydis was silent, staring out at the sea, so Hekja wondered why Freydis had bothered to call her over. Finally Freydis pointed at a bird, high overhead.

Hekja squinted upward, into the bright light.

"Does that mean we are near to land again?"

Freydis shook her head. "No. It's an albatross. That bird will fly further than any ship can sail." She smiled. "My father asked Leif once, when we were children, what bird he'd like to be. Leif said a raven, and my father clapped him on the back, and gave him a new sword the next time the traders called."

Hekja frowned. "I don't understand. Why was he pleased that Leif wanted to be a raven?"

"I forget you don't know our stories." Freydis gazed at the horizon. "Floki Vilgerdson discovered Iceland with his ravens. He carried them on his boat, and when he was past the Faroe Islands, he let one go. It flew straight back to the islands, and so he kept on sailing."

Freydis looked at Hekja, to see if she understood. Hekja frowned. "You mean, the nearest land was there, so that's where they flew?"

"Exactly," said Freydis, pleased. "Floki sailed on. Then he let another raven go. It flew high, up into the sky, as high as a bird could fly. But it saw no land, so it flew back down onto his boat. And Floki sailed on. Finally he let a third bird go. This one flew on and on and it was not flying in the direction of the islands. So Floki knew there must be land that way. He followed the raven and found Iceland."

"And that is why Leif wanted to be a raven," said Hekja slowly.

Freydis nodded. "My father never asked me what

bird I'd like to be. Why bother with a girl? But I told him anyway."

"An albatross?" asked Hekja.

"Good girl," said Freydis briefly.

Freydis was silent after that. Finally Hekja said, "I'd like to be an eagle."

"Would you? Why?"

"Because they see everything," said Hekja slowly. "No matter what happens below, an eagle can fly high above it all."

"But eagles hunt as well," said Freydis, amused. "Yes, an eagle would suit you. You didn't scream, back in the storm, as a woman is supposed to do at danger. You didn't even shriek when the iceberg's nearly dragged us down."

The albatross was just a speck now, riding the wind far beyond them. There was a new expression on Freydis's face as she watched it go, an almost wistful look.

At last she said, "Every time I look out at the ocean, I wonder what land there is beyond it, somewhere past the line where the sky meets the sea. My father found a new land and so did my brother. But I am a woman. I had to argue even to accompany my brother and my husband back to Norway, to trade the furs that Leif found in his new land. But one day . . ."

Hekja said curiously, "One day what?"

Freydis smiled at her. It was a different smile from all that she had given before. Those were smiles as

Freydis challenged the world, and laughed at it. But this was a real smile for Hekja.

"One day," she said softly, "I will follow the albatross, not the raven. I will find another land, just like my father did."

Something in Freydis's words had touched Hekja's soul. Even as she grieved her people's death and cursed her situation, Hekja too was dreaming of new lands and of wonders past the wall of the horizon.

Chapter 15

A Land of Snow

And then one day the clouds on the horizon glittered in the sun, and Hekja realized they weren't clouds at all. It was land. Hekja waited for the gray to turn to green. Instead the land grew whiter the closer they sailed.

Freydis was up in her usual place, by the prow. Hekja plucked up her courage and made her way over to her.

"Excuse me, mistress," she said. The word felt strange on her tongue. But that was the way Hikki spoke to Freydis, so Hekja supposed it was the way she should talk too.

Freydis glanced at her. "What is it?"

Hekja pointed out at the white land on the horizon. "Where is the green?"

Freydis grinned. "That was my father's trick," she said. There was pride in her voice. "He knew settlers wouldn't come to a place called Snowland. So he called his new land 'Greenland' and four hundred followed him, in twenty-five ships. Fourteen of those ships made it to shore."

"What happened to the other ships?"

Freydis shrugged. "They were lost in a storm, or turned back."

"What happened to the people?"

Freydis still gazed out at the distant land. Hekja thought she would have been happy to see land so close, but she was frowning. "They drowned."

"Do . . . do you think the people on the other ships who were with us drowned, too?"

Freydis gave her laugh. "Perhaps. I doubt Leif has drowned, though. The fish would spit him out. Besides, they call him Leif the Lucky."

The wind freshened suddenly. It came from the shore. It was warmer than the ocean wind, but it still smelled of ice, old ice, that had sat frozen perhaps since the world was made.

"Is the land all snow then?" Hekja demanded. She felt her hopes of escape begin to wither. If Greenland was a land of snow in summer, what must it be like in winter? How could she and Snarf survive by themselves in a land like this?

"There is snow and ice all year to the north, and in the high country. But in summer there is enough grass for sheep and goats and cattle."

Hekja frowned. She had never heard the words "sheep" and "goats" before. She would have to ask Hikki what they meant, later. Freydis had a closed look, as though she no longer wished to talk.

By midday the coast itself was visible, with deep bays the Vikings called fiords slashed into the high, fierce cliffs. Now Hekja could finally see some green, a thin rim around the shore. But the inland was high and white, with only the steep cliffs free of ice.

The land looked fierce, thought Hekja, a fitting place for Vikings. Where were all the people? Snarf barked beside her, excited by the smells of land.

Suddenly she smelled it. Smoke! So there were people in this frozen land! Even smoke smelled different here. She peered up at the cliffs, trying to see what lay beyond, but whatever lay above them was hidden from view.

The water looked strange too, more like milk than sea, and at times it sparkled, like stars that floated in the ripples.[14]

The wind had died down as they glided further into the fiord. The sails fell slack. The men pushed and pulled at the oars at either end of the ship. Hekja hadn't realized a fiord could be so big, or cliffs so high, great slabs of rock that looked about to slide into the milky sea.

Finally she glimpsed a break in the cliffs, a tiny beach of tumbled rocks with green hills above it. There was even a pier—a stone track out into the water, where a ship could sit and unload its goods

---

[14] The glacier at the end of the fiord ground the rocks to dust—it's called glacial flour. This is what made the water look milky and made it sparkle in sunlight.

without the people getting wet.

At the other end of the ship Thorvard gave a yell. "Home!"

"Home," repeated Freydis. But her face had lost its brightness.

"Hold her steady!" bellowed Thorvard. He threw one of the ropes, thick as a man's arm, around a big rock on the pier. The big ship drew close, as gently as a calf nudging its mother. Thorvard pulled the rope tighter, then looped it around some more.

The ship was home.

Two of the men shoved a thick plank across to the pier. Everyone was cheering, or chattering, hauling belongings from the pile. Hekja and Snarf sat forgotten. Freydis stepped onto the land first, then Thorvard, and then the others, till only Hekja and Snarf were left.

"Arf?" asked Snarf inquiringly.

Hekja shrugged. She had been waiting for someone to give her orders, but it seemed no one could be bothered. A new thrall and a dog were of little importance now. She stood up and tried to ignore the pounding of her heart.

Suddenly there were voices from the hill above them, shouts and laughter. People raced down to the shore. Children first, running down the grassy hill and onto the stone pier. Everyone was yelling and hugging the new arrivals, peering into the ship and asking questions.

One young boy caught sight of Snarf and nudged his friend. Hekja grabbed the scruff of his neck and held on tight, in case he ran on shore without her.

Now the adults came, giant men with flowing hair or plaits and shaggy beards, with woolen caps instead of helmets. There were women, too, strong-shouldered women in long dresses like Freydis wore, though these women wore hoods or scarves. Most wore aprons, too, and some had bracelets of gold or bronze or silver.

Now the crowd parted. A man strode down the hill. His hair hung like snow down to his shoulders, and his beard was snowy as well. Once he must have been a giant man, big even for these Vikings. Now his skin hung about him, as though he had shrunk. He walked with the aid of a great stick that was carved like a dragon at the top, embellished with eyes of green stone and all inlaid with brass.

The chief back in the village was not like this. You knew this was a chief without being told.

The others all moved aside for him, except for Freydis. And suddenly Hekja saw her eyes were like the man's, though his were faded, as though all that they had seen had worn them out; the shape of her face was his, too.

No one paid any attention to Hekja. Then Hikki beckoned from the pier. "Come," he said impatiently.

Snarf bounded off first. Suddenly he staggered.

"Snarf!" Hekja darted onto the pier—and staggered just as he had. Her legs were waiting for the ground to go up and down after so many days at sea.

"This must be Erik the Red," Hikki whispered when Hekja joined him in the crowd. "Though he is red no longer."

Hekja ignored him, staring at the man.

"Well, daughter?" Hekja had expected a great roar, but the big man's voice was hoarse.

"It is very well, Father," said Freydis calmly. "A good voyage, and much profit."

"I know. Your brother landed two days before you."

Freydis's eyes narrowed, but she kept her face steady. "Always Leif the Lucky," she said. "It seems I owe him a shawl. Did the other ships arrive safe as well?"

"All but one. Njal Thorbjorgsson's ship was lost and all it carried. Except for him, the crew were saved."

In Hekja's village the loss of any man at sea would cause an outcry, with women weeping. But Freydis only nodded. "It was a good voyage," she said. "And a safe one."

Hekja waited for her to tell her father about the storm and Snarf barking at the icebergs. But she didn't.

The men were unloading the ship now, with Thorvard bellowing orders. Freydis began to climb the hill with her father. Had she forgotten them?

"Woof!" Snarf's bark was louder than Thorvard's

yells. Freydis looked around and spied Hekja still standing on the pier.

"Follow me," she said absently. Somehow she looked smaller here on land, especially next to her father.

Erik the Red raised an eyebrow at her. "A new thrall?"

"Leif didn't tell you?" Freydis grinned suddenly. "A storm drove us to shelter, and there was a village. Leif tried to catch this girl, but she outran him."

"Outran Leif!" The old man gave a shout of laughter. "A girl like that!"

"And now she is mine. I stopped her with the flat of my sword."

"Your sword?" The old man glared at her. "By thunder, your mother never wielded a sword in her life!"

"Nor did she ever go a-Viking. Mother died bearing your sons. Her only journey was following you here."

"As it should be," grumbled the man, and for the first time he sounded truly old. "And when will you have sons?"

"When I am ready," said Freydis coolly. "And that is a matter for my husband and myself, not for my father."

"If Thorvard were half a man—" Erik broke off, as Thorvard came up behind them, his arms burdened with a bale of wool, almost as large as he was, though he carried it easily. Hekja wondered what Erik meant by "half a man." Thorvard was almost twice the size of any villager.

It was impossible to tell if he had heard what his father-in-law had said. He just nodded and said, "Sir. I'm glad to see you well."

Erik snorted. "Only one leg that works properly and breath that gives out if I so much as climb a hill, and he calls me well. I'm well enough, I suppose."

They had reached the top of the hill above the fiord now. Hekja had never dreamed that even a village could be so big. There was a great longhouse, as big as all the village huts put together, made of stone with a roof of turf. Smaller buildings clustered about it, each one bigger than anything she'd known. There were fields with fences of twined wattles[15] filled with strange new animals. There were grain fields, too, and gardens filled with greens, familiar plants like kale and garlic, but others she had never seen before.

And there were lines of dried fish flapping, cods' tongues and whale liver, and other meat and hides hanging up to dry as well. There were people everywhere. And the smells, so strong after the many days at sea!

And above all this were the heights of blinding snow and blue-white ice, and lower hills of green, with stunted trees with dappled leaves.[16] The sun

---

[15] small branches

[16] small birch trees (There were no big conifers in Greenland for roof beams or boats.)

hung on the horizon, bathing it all in a golden glow.

"Arf arf!" For a moment Hekja thought Snarf was also responding to the strangeness. Then she noticed a dog, almost as large as him, bounding their way. Snarf wagged his tail.

"Bright Eyes!" cried Erik. The dog bounded up to him.

"Arf," barked Snarf again. Hekja grabbed him. She wasn't sure how Erik would feel if Snarf sniffed his dog.

The dog ignored Snarf, and the other humans, too, and crouched down by her master.

Erik bent and fondled her ears. "Good dog," he said absently. "Well, daughter, will you come to the big house?"

She shook her head. "We will go to our own, Father."

"But a feast tonight!" ordered Erik. "There has to be a feast."

Freydis gave a laugh like his. "A feast tonight," she agreed. "I thought you would have done your feasting when Leif arrived."

"We waited for your coming," said Erik gruffly, and Hekja saw that for all his disapproval Erik loved her.

Freydis smiled suddenly. "Come," she said to Hekja. She and Snarf followed Freydis across the fields.

Chapter 16

The New Home

Freydis's farm was on the other side of the fiord, through cow pasture. Hekja felt a pang of homesickness at their familiar chomp, chomp, chomping, and Snarf tried to sniff at every cowpat.

The next fields had stranger animals, smaller than Snarf but hairier. "Sheep," said Thorvard briefly, smiling at Hekja's obvious amazement. "Where wool comes from."

Raina and Reena, the chief's daughters, had worn woolen dresses, made from cloth traded for a side of smoked beef. But Hekja had always worn cowhide.

They walked over the crest of another hill, with a spring bubbling from its side. There were more buildings, none as large as Erik's, but still amazing to Hekja's eyes. Each one was made of stone, with a high turf roof, all covered in grass even greener than the fields, as there were no cows up there to eat it.

There were what looked like storerooms, so many that she wondered if even Hikki's numbers could count them. There was one that looked like a dairy, with cheeses and butter barrels along its walls, and another giant empty one.

Finally they came to the biggest building of all.

It was almost as big as a hill, but long instead of round. Three of its walls were made of straw, and one of carved wood. Then suddenly the wood wall opened!

Hekja gasped. It was a door! The first wooden door that she had ever seen. Freydis ducked her head under the lintel and went inside, and so did Thorvard. Snarf lifted his leg on the corner of the house and produced a proprietary dribble, then he and Hekja followed.

It took a moment for her eyes to get used to the dimness indoors, after so many days in brightness on the sea. There were great white rafters[17] supporting the roof, and the walls were lined with wood, with webs of moss poking out here and there, so hardly a breath of outside air came in the house. The floor was dirt, swept hard and clean. Three fires flickered in a long, stone fire pit, halfway down the house. They smelled of wood and fish oil. Above the fire pit a great roast dangled on a metal chain, and above that was the smoke hole in the roof.

Beside the fire was a great carved chair. There were benches too, with sheepskins draped across them, and a big wooden table. More skins stitched

---

[17] whale bones

together hung from the roof beams at one end of the house, marking off a private room.

On a platform was a strange device[18] with a length of cloth draped over it, a ladder up to a loft, and two more doors with skins draped across their openings.[19]

"Welcome home, mistress!"

"It is good to be home, Gudrun," said Thorvard as an old woman with fat ankles waddled forward. Her face was as wrinkled as an empty sausage skin, her mouth shrunk and toothless, and her thin plaits gray. Saliva sprayed from her gums in her eagerness to talk.

There was a torrent of words after that, from Gudrun to Freydis, most of which Hekja found hard to understand. It seemed to be about the farm and people and animals, but too many words were new. Beside her Snarf sat on his haunches and stared at the roast meat, in case someone decided to take it away.

Finally Gudrun stopped talking. Freydis waved a hand at Hekja. "Gudrun, this is Hekja. She's a runner from the islands. I don't know what else she's good for. She may need training before you find her much use."

Gudrun peered shortsightedly at Hekja and ran her hand across Hekja's face as though examining her features. She looked down at Snarf dubiously.

---

[18] a loom, for weaving

[19] storerooms

"Arf," said Snarf. He rolled over at Gudrun's feet in his dead dog position. Hekja recognized his way of saying, "I am at your command."

Old Gudrun smiled and rubbed his tummy with her booted foot. Then she looked back at Hekja.

"Well, girl?" she demanded a bit indistinctly, as Thorvard and Freydis lifted the skins and went into their room at the other end of the house. "What can you do, hey?"

Hekja hesitated. "At home I minded the cows on the mountain. I made butter and cheese. I dried the fish with Ma and collected shellfish and—" Her voice broke off. She wouldn't cry. She wouldn't! But the tears ran nonetheless at the thought of home and Ma.

Hekja waited for Gudrun to laugh at her weakness, as Freydis might. But Gudrun patted her arm awkwardly instead with her age-spotted hand. "And where is your ma now, hey?" she asked gently.

Hekja shook her head. She made no other reply, but Gudrun understood. "Well," she said, even more gently, "there are cows to watch and cheese to make here. Perhaps your life won't be so different after all."

Hekja's face was wet. "You are a thrall, too?" she whispered.

Gudrun nodded. "All my life, and my mother's, too, and my grandmother, since the beginning of time. I came with the old master's wife from Iceland. But I've known others be taken from Ireland or the islands. You'll find it hard at first, but you'll get used to it. There's food enough and shelter. What more can we ask for, hey?"

Hekja said nothing. The old woman patted her arm. "Are you hungry? There's food if you like."

"Arf!" said Snarf enthusiastically. He'd recognized the word.

Hekja shook her head.

"Arf," Snarf barked again. He sniffed toward the hanging roast, as though it was a hare he'd hunted.

Gudrun laughed, and patted his head. "You're hungrier than you know, after all those days of dried fish," she said to Hekja comfortingly. "You'll feel better when you've eaten."

She made her way to a cupboard—its door carved with tinier shapes than Hekja had thought a knife could make—and pulled out some cheese and a barley loaf, just like what she used to eat at home, but much more plentiful, and a large hunk of cold meat, too. Snarf knelt before her and slobbered on the floor.

Gudrun pulled at the small knife on the chain on her belt and hacked off some pieces of meat and cheese. She handed them to Hekja, then threw the rest of the meat to Snarf.

Gudrun was right. The food stopped Hekja's tears. And meat! All the meat she wanted, and meat for Snarf, too, given so easily by one who was a thrall as well. So far Greenland was better than she had hoped.

After Hekja had finished eating, Gudrun ordered her to the outbuildings, to help store the goods that had been unloaded from the ship. The size of everything confused Hekja at first, so Gudrun told her to sit and wipe the new weapons and tools with fish oil. Meanwhile the men carried the ship to its cradle in the giant empty shed, where it would be stripped of barnacles and caulked with rotted birch leaves to stop the water coming through the cracks.

Snarf bounded at everyone's sides, as though he was making sure that he was everywhere at once—in case a wolf attacked or an iceberg decided to invade the land. He kept an eye out for places he'd missed lifting his leg on and snapped at passing butterflies or the tail feathers of the hens.

It was late by the time everyone had finished, though the sun still hovered near to the horizon. Despite all that had happened, it was still not far from midsummer, when the days were longest.

By now the smell of meat roasting for the feast floated across from Erik's farm. It seemed that only Freydis and Thorvard were going to go. Freydis changed her dress and put on a necklace and more bangles and different brooches made of shining metal and sparkling stones. Then she and Thorvard walked across the fields to Erik's without a word to Hekja. Freydis had more important things to do now than talk to a thrall.

"Here, boy! Sit!" Gudrun beamed at Hekja. "What a good dog he is! He comes when he is called!"

Hekja smiled tiredly. Snarf came so eagerly because he smelled the roast hanging from its chain.

"Good dog," said Gudrun approvingly, patting his head. "Do you know how to cook meat?" she asked Hekja.

Hekja shook her head. "I can cook barley bread, and fish stew. But I've never roasted meat before."

"Just keep the meat turning, then, and turn the pot so it doesn't get too hot, or the pudding will burn. You understand?"

"Yes," said Hekja. She poked the great roast of meat carefully. It spun gently as she touched it, and juice dripped down into the pot of grains and greens below.

Then a group of men came in—two thralls, and three freemen who worked on the farm. They looked curiously at Hekja, but asked no questions. Hekja was grateful. Her tongue felt thick with tiredness, and she was afraid that if anyone asked about where she came from, she might cry again. The men sat by the smoky fire and talked about straying sheep and a sow that almost crushed a piglet—more words that Hekja didn't know. The two thralls also spoke to each other in a language the others didn't seem to understand.

"They are from Ireland," Gudrun whispered as she passed with a platter of barley bread. Hekja nodded, though the word "Ireland" made no sense.

Gudrun put the meat down onto a platter and sliced it up. Her portion was minced into tiny bits, as she had no teeth to chew with. There were slabs for everyone else and the meaty bones and scraps for Snarf. Snarf gulped the meat scraps then rolled over, panting, so Gudrun could scratch his belly with her booted foot.

Each person had a spoon to eat the pudding from the pot. Hekja had never seen spoons so small. She watched how the others used them before dipping in her own.

The pudding was the best thing she had ever eaten, rich with cream and meat juices, sweet with fruit and honey, the soft grains melting with the greens. Even toothless Gudrun was able to eat it with ease, as it needed no chewing at all.

The fire burned low, till it was only coals. The house was dark, except for the twilight through the door. The men rolled themselves in sheepskins from the benches and went to sleep beside the glowing fire. Gudrun nodded to Hekja to do the same.

She felt stranger than she ever had—stranger even than on the boat. But she was too tired to stay awake, and the sheepskin was the softest, warmest thing that she had ever felt. She fell asleep with Snarf by her side, and didn't even notice when he rose to investigate more smells from outside, including Erik's bitch.

Even when Freydis and Thorvard returned, she

didn't wake, till Thorvard stumbled against one of the sleeping men, then kicked him drunkenly.

"Wake up, you lazy louts!" cried Thorvard as he staggered past.

Hekja started to her feet, but Thorvard and Freydis were already in their room. The great wood door had been left open. Outside the sun was rising above the storerooms, and the hens were running after insects. The sheep were bleating, and the cows calling to be milked.

Her life in Greenland had begun.

Chapter 17

Greenland

They ate leftovers for breakfast—cold meat and bread and fermented milk. Gudrun watched while Hekja milked the cows, who stood with their heads through the stalls and munched at a handful of hay.

Finally Gudrun nodded. "You know what you are about, girl," she said, hauling herself off the milking stool and onto her swollen feet. "Finish the milking yourself, then take the cows out beyond the barley fields and keep them straying. I'll ring the bell when it's time to bring them in."

"What's a bell?" asked Hekja, stumbling over the new word.

Gudrun shook her head. "What place have you been living in, hey? A bell is . . . a bell is . . . when you hear a loud noise, girl, a ding-ding-ding, then you'll know it's time to milk again."

"Arf," said Snarf, wagging his tail in case Gudrun had another hunk of meat with her. She patted him on the way out and slipped him a bit of barley bread from her apron.

One by one the cows were milked. A man came to take the buckets of milk back to the dairy. Hekja was just stripping[20] the last cow—a big red beast with horns that could lift a deer—when she heard a whistle behind her.

"Where is that blasted hound!" It was Thorvard. "Here, boy! Here!" He grabbed Snarf by the scruff of the neck and pulled him to his feet. Snarf grunted in surprise, then flopped back down again, onto his tummy, to show he'd do whatever was wanted.

"What are you doing!" Hekja leaped to her feet so suddenly she knocked over the bucket of milk. The cow pulled its head out of the wooden stall to watch them curiously.

Thorvard stared at her. "Get on with your milking, girl!" He bent to haul Snarf up again.

"No! Stop it! You'll hurt him!"

Thorvard struck her across the face. Her eyes watered, and she staggered, but she didn't cry out.

Snarf growled, deep in his throat. He could accept orders from other humans, but no one was allowed to touch Hekja while he was near.

Hekja put her arms around Snarf's great neck. "Leave him alone!" she yelled.

For a moment she thought Thorvard would strike her again. But then he began to laugh. "The dog is as

---

[20] getting the last of the milk from the cow's udder

big as you!" he roared. "And you think you will protect him!"

"What's happening here!" It was Freydis.

Thorvard stopped laughing, but his grin was as wide as a cheese. "It's your new thrall here. It seems she objects to my disciplining the dog. Perhaps you would like to fight me for him, hey, thrall?"

Freydis looked at Hekja coolly. "I thought we had this out on the ship. This dog is mine now." Her words were hard, but her eyes were amused.

Hekja shook her head, confused. "I . . . will fight . . . if you want me to," she stammered. "But you are not to hurt Snarf."

Suddenly Thorvard seemed to understand. He lifted Hekja's chin with his fingers. "I was joking, girl. But the dog needs to be trained if he is to be of use."

"What will he be used for?" demanded Hekja.

Thorvard glanced at Freydis. "She doesn't give in, does she?" There was admiration in his voice now. "He is a hunting dog. He needs to learn the hunting commands. Do you really want him to sit with you all day, a fine dog like that, while you watch the cows?"

Hekja was silent for a moment. Then she said slowly, "In our village the chief's dog did what the chief commanded at the hunt. But I never knew how to teach Snarf what to do."

"I know dogs, girl," said Thorvard. "My dog, Silvertail, died on our way to Norway. I will train your dog well."

"My dog?" inquired Hekja. She wasn't sure if she had heard correctly.

"Your dog," Thorvard said seriously. "But you are my thrall, so he is mine as well. Understood?"

"I understand," said Hekja.

Thorvard shook his head. "What is the world coming to? Making bargains with a thrall." But he was grinning.

Freydis looked at Hekja. "I think I may have won more than I realized when I captured you from my brother."

And so Snarf went to work with Thorvard, learning to come when he whistled, to sit when he clicked his fingers, to run at his heels until he gave the signal to chase. He learned to follow the scent that Thorvard chose, and not to be distracted; to bring game back, and drop it at his feet; and to point properly when he sensed an animal in the bushes.

Finally Thorvard took him hunting. They hunted polar bear for their thick white coats, and walrus, prized for their ivory tusks. They tracked seals and eider ducks and auk, giant birds with precious feathers who were too docile to even run away. The soft duck feathers were as valuable as the waterproof sealskins, and earned much silver from Norwegian traders.

After every hunt, as the men and women of Brattahlid streamed out to greet the hunters, Snarf would sniff out Hekja. She would hug him, and he would lick her face as though to say, "No matter how far I have hunted, I am still your dog." Even when Thorvard whistled for him the next day, Snarf would wait till Hekja gave him her own signal that he should go.

During the days she missed Snarf, but life was busy for Hekja, too. Freydis managed her thralls to make sure the cows were getting fat for winter, or as much as this icy land would allow. They milked twice a day, made butter, cheese and skyr[21], and sheared the sheep.

The farm had been a gift to Freydis from Erik on her wedding day, and it prospered under her care. It was Freydis who oversaw the ploughing and the harvest. She saw the grain ground into flour, or parched and stored in barrels for the winter. It was Freydis who ordered the fish hung and dried, the bear and deer meat salted, the whale blubber boiled for oil, the cods' tongues pickled, the onions hung in bundles in the shed, the moss and rose root dried and stored for when the sunlight vanished for the year.

Gudrun helped with all of this, but she was getting old. Once Freydis found that Hekja knew how to handle herself—especially once she learned that Hekja would work with no one watching her, and pass on her orders to the men as well—more and more was left to her.

---

[21] a fermented milk drink

Chapter 18

Strange Ships

But there were quiet times, too. Hekja could sit with Snarf up on the hills, watching the cows, just as they had watched them back on the great mountain at home. Hekja often saw Hikki as he jogged across the hills with his messages to other farms, but he never stopped to talk.

At times like this, if she blocked out Hikki and the strong smell if the ice, she could almost imagine she was home. Soon Ma would come with a barley cake hot from the stone, or Bran might stride across the hill. . . .

Somehow Hekja found that she was singing again. The tune was old, but the words seemed to come from some unknown part within herself.

"The birds fly together,
The deer run with friends,
But here I am lonely,
There my past ends.

"My words end in silence,
No one understands,
My life or my language,
The heart of my land.

"I once walked with friendship,
I once sang with joy,
But here I'm a slave,
In a stranger's employ."

The words echoed across the empty hills. Suddenly Snarf lifted up his nose and sang as well.

"Howwwwl!"

Hekja stopped singing. Snarf hadn't tried to sing with her since the days in the far-off hut by the shore, with Ma and all the precious familiar things around them.

"Oh, Snarf!" she cried. And suddenly she was weeping, her arms linked around his neck, snuffling into his long fur.

Snarf twisted around and tried to lick the tears from her face, which made her laugh, as well as cry. Finally she sat up, her arm about him, and looked out at the cows, the farm below, and the milky fiord with its icebergs bumbling through the waves.

"Sometimes . . . sometimes," she said, "I think I can't stand it anymore. There isn't even anyone who knows my land, except for you and Hikki, who ignores me. Every time I see an eagle or a wild goose,

I think, If only I were like you, I could fly back home."

"Arf," said Snarf comfortingly. "Arf arf."

Hekja wiped her nose on the back of her hand. "Sometimes I think I hate them all. They are the people who killed Ma, killed my village! But other times . . ."

"Woof!" Snarf barked. But this was his warning call.

Someone was coming. It was Gudrun, puffing her way up the hill, a basket in her hand. Hekja wiped her eyes quickly and ran back down. "You shouldn't have come so far!" she cried.

Gudrun's face was red, but she smiled, even as she puffed. "It will do me good to get out," she said. "There was a time when I used to spend days up here, like you. I thought, I'll just see the world from the hills once again and bring the girl some food."

Gudrun sat down and opened the basket.

"Strawberries!" cried Hekja.

Gudrun grinned. "I saved some for you from the mistress's dinner." She laid out more food on the wiry grass. There was smoked whale tongue, too, and eggs baked with cream and honey, as well as a large bone for Snarf, still with good meat on it.

"Woof," said Snarf, wagging his tail appreciatively. He grabbed the bone and took it aside to look after it.

Hekja ate while Gudrun talked. Gudrun liked to talk. Hekja sometimes wondered if she had saved up her words till Hekja came.

Once Gudrun talked of the time that Master Erik

caught a live polar bear and kept it in a metal cage. He had it shipped to Norway to astonish the folks there and then sold it for a large sum of silver.

Another time she told her mother's tale of the Starving Year in Iceland, when the great volcano belched out clouds of ash all across the land and the ground trembled as though to shake all humans off its shores. That winter lasted for an entire year, and all but the strongest died.

"Was that why Master Erik came here?" Hekja had asked. "Because of the volcano?"

Gudrun shook her head. "He killed men unlawfully, in Norway, and then in Iceland, too. His lands were confiscated, and he was exiled for three years. That is when he discovered Greenland. But this is a good place, in spite of the cold, with enough land for everyone. In my grandmother's day in Iceland, a man could claim all he could walk around in a day while carrying a flaming torch, and a woman could claim all she could walk in a day leading a two-year-old heifer. But now all the good land there has been taken."

This time, as they sat on the green hill and ate strawberries, Gudrun told of the Greenland winter when she lost her teeth. "The snow came early and stayed late," said Gudrun, happily remembering what had once been horror, "and when the men went out in boats, there were no fish for their nets. Master Erik wanted to kill the stock, while there was still meat left on them to eat. But my mistress said no. If we ate the stock, we would have no food for the next year. One by one my teeth fell out," said Gudrun. "Every morning there was another to spit onto my furs. I even sucked the furs, I was so hungry. We ate the reindeer moss; we ground the fish bones in the quern. Then, just as I thought I'd see the floor through my hands, the traders came. Their great boat had a huge store of grain and malt and all good things that Master Erik could buy with his wealth of silver. Oh, we ate and ate, and then were sick, and then we ate again. But since that time . . ."

Hekja gasped.

"What is it, child?" cried Gudrun.

Hekja was looking out to sea. "No," she whispered. "No!"

Gudrun peered out to sea with her faded eyes. "What can you see?"

"Ships!" cried Hekja. "Ships!"

"They'll be hunting whales, then," said Gudrun, puzzled at Hekja's distress. "The master took his harpoon and the sealskin floats from the storeroom this morning."

"No! These ships are different! They've come to attack us, just like before!" cried Hekja. "I have to tell Freydis!"

Suddenly she was running, almost as fast as a bird could fly, down the hill. Snarf bounded after her.

"Hekja, come back!" called Gudrun.

But Hekja kept on running. Down the hill, over

the grass, which was scattered with cow droppings and sheep dung, then past the barley field, then the sheep yard. The men stared at her as she ran past, and some cried out. But Hekja didn't stop.

Into the courtyard she ran, past the flapping lines of drying fish. The hens scattered, squawking and dropping feathers.

"Freydis! Freydis!" yelled Hekja.

That was not how a thrall addressed her mistress, but Hekja didn't care.

"Freydis!"

"What in thunder is all the yelling about?" Freydis pushed open the dairy door and stood staring.

"Arf!" Snarf leaped over a startled hen. "Arf!"

"Freydis!" panted Hekja. "I'm sorry, I mean, mistress . . ."

"What is it?" Then Freydis added, "Shut that dog up!"

"Ships! Five of them, out on the horizon!"

"Five?" Freydis looked interested, not alarmed.

"Aren't they invaders?" cried Hekja.

Freydis laughed. "Oh, I see, you have sounded the alarm. Well, thank you, I suppose, but there was no need. Who would dare come a-Viking here, to Erik's den? No, they'll be traders, from Iceland perhaps, or even Norway. I must go and change. You," she added, to a staring thrall, "go and watch the cows. And you, Hekja, wash the cow dirt off your face. I think"— Freydis gave a smile—"you will be needed."

Chapter 19

The Traders

Freydis soon came out, wearing a clean apron and a red and green silk scarf about her head. She had a gold chain hanging around her neck and her best brooches. She hurried across the fields, down to the pier. Others were heading that way, too.

Gudrun arrived back with the basket, panting and exclaiming that Hekja was not to worry. By now Hekja was embarrassed to think she had panicked at the sight of ships on the sea.

No one had told Hekja she was allowed to go down to the pier as well. So she and Gudrun collected the eggs and changed the weights and wrappings on the cheeses. Each time she peered out to the courtyard, Hekja could see the ships coming further and further up the fiord. They were like the one that Hekja and Snarf had traveled in, with store boats bobbing behind them, laden with lengths of timber and barrels.

"What is in the barrels?" asked Hekja as she

dipped the cheesecloth in salty water, a Greenlander trick that prevented mould.

Old Gudrun shrugged. "Grain, perhaps, or cooking pots."

"But we grow barley here! And oats as well." Oats made a softer porridge and bread than barley, and Hekja had grown fond of it.

"Not enough to see us through the winter, not if you want to keep your belly full! That is why the masters trade, hey? The traders bring wood, too, big lengths, not like the trees out there." Gudrun gestured at the stunted trees up on the hill. "Trees don't grow big enough for roof beams or barrels in this cold land."

Hekja wrinkled her forehead. "But why do the traders bring things here? As a gift?"

"To get other goods in return, of course! Did you never have traders in your village? They get good furs and walrus ivory and walrus rope, yes, and stockfish and whale oil. Ah, but you should have seen the furs Master Leif brought back from Vinland. Master Leif is richer even than his father now."

Gudrun glanced out the door. "They have landed already! We will have some excitement soon, hey? There'll be feasting and who knows what else." She shot Hekja a look. "You be careful, girl."

"But they're traders, not invaders. Freydis—I mean the mistress—said not to worry," said Hekja, puzzled.

"That may be," said Gudrun, "but when men have been at sea, and the ale is flowing—you be careful, child. Stay out of the way, if you can, so no one notices you. You understand?"

Hekja bit her lip, remembering some of the things she had seen when her village had been invaded. She nodded. "I wouldn't let any Norseman touch me."

"You may not get a choice," said Gudrun dryly.

"I can outrun them," declared Hekja. "Like I did before."

Gudrun looked shocked for a moment. Then she shook her head. "A thrall takes what is handed out to her."

She shook her head as Hekja shrugged. "No, child, I am quite serious. If a master wants you, you can't stop him. If you try—if you run—it will be the worse for you. A master can chop your hand off, or kill you if that is his pleasure. The only way for a thrall to be safe is to make sure she stays out of the way, especially when the drink flows freely. Why do you think the mistress hasn't given you a good dress?"

Hekja stared at her. Gudrun nodded. "The mistress is wise. In that dress you look like a child, not a woman. The men will go for better game than a barbarian who's dressed in tatters. But you take care. I knew a girl once . . ." Gudrun bit her lip.

"What girl?" demanded Hekja.

"Dear girl, I tell you these things only so you will be careful. She was a thrall, from Ireland, when the old mistress was alive. She had a baby, and who the father was no one knew or cared, except its mother. But winter was coming, and food was short. So one night the mistress ordered the baby taken out and left on the rocks."

Hekja stared. "What happened to it?"

"It died," said Gudrun simply. "And its mother cast herself off the cliff, down by Erik's farm. See, you can see the spot over there, by that twisted tree. And no one cared, for she was just a thrall."

Hekja lifted her chin. She whistled softly. Snarf came up to her and she hugged him close. "I am only a thrall in their eyes, not in mine," she declared defiantly.

Gudrun looked worried. But she only said, "Try not to get noticed."

The crowd was heading up the hill now, toward Erik's farm. Thorvard broke from them, and strode across the fields. "You, girl!" he yelled to Hekja. His hands were red with dried whale blood—he had been cutting blubber down on the beach and had obviously had no time to wash when the traders arrived.

"Yes, master?" said Hekja obediently.

"The mistress wants you, over at her father's . . . Now!" he added, as Hekja failed to move at once.

Hekja handed Gudrun the last of the cheese wrappings.

"Remember!" hissed Gudrun. "Take care."

Hekja nodded. She ran across the fields, her bare

feet slapping against the ground. The Greenlanders wore leather boots strapped around their ankles. Most of the thralls had them too, but no one had given Hekja any to wear. no one had even given her warmer clothes, except for the cowskin cloak Freydis had given her on board the ship.

"There you are!" Freydis stood with Erik and Leif, examining great lengths of wood. "Father, if this girl can't outrun Leif's runner, I will give him my best cow."

The old man looked Hekja up and down. "You've seen her run? She has the legs for it, at any rate. But will she last the distance and find her way?"

"She will," said Freydis confidently.

Hekja looked from one to the other, but didn't speak. She already had learned that speaking out of turn would earn her a slap across the ear.

"Hikki!" roared Erik suddenly.

The runner stepped out from one of the store sheds. "Yes, master?"

"I want you to take a message. It's two days' sail north, but you will run it. Understand?"

"Yes, master," said Hikki confidently. He shot a glance at Hekja. "I can run faster than any ship can sail."

"We'll see," said Erik.

"What is the message and where am I taking it?" asked Hikki.

"The farm is due north of here, the first one that you come to up the coast, as far up a fiord as this one. The message is for my youngest son, Thorstein Eriksson. Tell him: 'The traders have come. Bring your furs and join the feast." Understood?"

"Yes, master." Hikki glanced at the sun. "I will need dried fish, so I may eat as I run. Then I will be gone."

"One moment," ordered Erik. He nodded at Hikki. "This girl is a runner too."

"Her?" Hikki looked at Hekja in astonishment. "Girls can't be runners!" he protested.

One of the traders had overheard. He was young, only a few years older than Hekja, with hair the same shade as the butter she had churned that morning. He stared at Hekja, which made her remember that she had forgotten to wash the cow dirt off her face, as Freydis had told her to. "A girl runner?" he asked curiously. "Do the women in your country run too?"

Hekja shook her head. Suddenly she wished she had proper shoes, and a woolen dress, and a hairbrush like Freydis's so she too could pull her hair back into plaits.

"I've never heard of a girl runner," said the young man, pulling out some dried meat from his pouch and feeding it to the delighted Snarf. "Surely they don't have the strength."

"Perhaps there are things you haven't heard of,

Snorri the Skald,"[22] said Freydis calmly. "Maybe girls are more capable than you think. Hekja, I want you to take the message too. And if my brother's runner gets there first, you will be beaten."

Hekja met her eyes. "I'll run as fast as I can," she said. "I don't need a beating to make me run."

Snorri gave a shout of laughter. "There is no way a girl can beat a man! Uncle Nils!" he called to one of the other traders. "This girl is a runner!"

It's like I'm a strange beetle in the grass, to be exclaimed over, thought Hekja.

"Girls cannot run," said Hikki flatly. "Their skirts get in the way."

Hekja glanced at Freydis. Freydis smiled. "Run!" she said softly.

Hekja hesitated. Surely she should take dried fish too, and maybe water. But, then she caught Freydis's eye. This way she would have a head start over Hikki!

Hekja ran, sprinting across the fields, with the men's laughter echoing behind, and Snarf leaping at her heels.

---

[22] Skalds were renowned poets, historians, and singers. The stories they chanted were for entertainment, beauty, and to record the past.

Chapter 20

The Race

Once out of sight, Hekja slowed down. She knew there was no way she could keep that pace for long.

Where was she supposed to run to? North, Erik had said, and hug the coast. That should be easy enough, thought Hekja. And Hikki said that he could make the run in less than two days. Surely she could run that long.

But fast enough to beat Hikki? Hikki had run messages for years. He was used to finding his way across this country. Somehow Hekja knew that there was more to being a runner than just putting one foot in front of another.

She was now past the familiar hills where she had herded the cattle. She crested another hill and suddenly there was a fiord in front of her, a deep gash of rock and cliffs with the waves crashing down below. Snarf began to bound down between the rocks, but Hekja called him back.

"This way! Good dog! We need to go around, not down!"

"Arf," said Snarf happily, as though this was the best game he'd played for days. He galloped along the cliff edge, just as Hekja caught sight of Hikki, in the distance.

He was wearing a strange shift, just two lengths of cloth tied together at the sides and fastened between his legs, so his arms and legs were free to run, and he had a sealskin pack over one shoulder. He was running further inland, so he had missed the fiord altogether, loping along as though he had done this all his life. Which, of course, he had.

Hikki waved and grinned, but didn't slow down. In a few heartbeats he was gone.

Hekja bit her lip. Hikki was ahead of her now, and likely to remain so. But all she could do was try her best.

Over rocks and up cliffs she ran, scrabbling at the loose gravel and sliding down the slippery rock faces. Several times she had to stop and go back and find another route, each time keeping the smell and sound of the sea to her left. And all the time the thought pounded through her brain: Hikki knows how to judge the land. He won't have to double back like this. We will never catch him. Never.

Hekja had seen one of the thralls beaten, when he had left an axe out in the rain to rust. There had been blood down his back and face.

"I would rather run forever than be whipped," muttered Hekja under her breath. "Run up into the ice, so the ice giants can catch me, and freeze me forever. . . ."

The sun sank below the horizon. The summer twilight filled the sky, dark enough for a few bright stars, but still bright enough for Hekja to find her way.

Hekja's breath came in long, deep pants and even Snarf was tired now.

Hekja ran her fingers through his fur. "We'll have to stop till it gets light. Do you think Hikki will run all night?"

Snarf scratched a flea instead of answering.

There was a clump of rocks a little way ahead, enough to shelter them from the chill breeze blowing up from the sea. Hekja wrapped herself around Snarf's warmth. The ground was hard and cold, and she hadn't even brought her cloak. But she was so tired that sleep came despite it all.

The first light woke her, the sun gleaming above the icy mountains. She was almost too stiff to move, and hungry, too. She had run for half a day and half a night, and it had been a long time since Gudrun's strawberries on the hill. Snarf was already snuffling around the rocks, hoping to find mice or lizards. But he followed her as soon as she began to run.

The shadows shrank and the day grew warmer, and the sun dried up the dew. There were streams to drink from, but hunger ate at her insides. Worse, it was slowing her down. Several times she stumbled, dizzy and unsure of where to put her feet.

Then suddenly Snarf stopped and sniffed the wind.

"Snarf! What is it?" Hekja whistled. "Come!"

Snarf whined. He'd come if she wanted him to. But there was something he wanted to investigate, down on the beach.

Hekja hesitated. "Go on then," she said. "I'll rest, just for a moment."

Snarf whined again, signaling Hekja to follow.

Hekja nodded and did as he asked.

There was an animal track between the rocks, which led them down to the sandy beach. And there it was—the carcass of a whale. It was as long as a farmhouse and almost as high.

Perhaps it had beached itself. Or maybe fishermen had brought it in. But certainly men had taken all the meat along the spine—the tide and ravens would never have picked it off so cleanly. The only meat left was right at the head. Hekja stuck her hand into the blowhole. The meat was still warm, still fresh. The fishermen could not have left it long ago.

The Irish thralls back at the farm had talked of whale feasts on the beach, where they ate the whale meat while it was warm and raw. She would never have considered eating raw blubber before, but Hekja was too hungry to care. This was food, and it would keep her going. No matter how bad it tasted, she would force it down.

Snarf tore at a piece of blubber and chewed it hungrily. Hekja tried to do the same, but without a knife it was impossible. Finally Hekja shared what Snarf had managed to tear off with his teeth. It tasted better than she had expected—tough but juicy. Best of all, it filled her belly and gave her enough strength to keep going.

Once she was full, she finally washed the blood from her hands and mouth in the cold seawater. Snarf wiped his mouth on the grass.

Then Hekja began to run again.

They ran all that day, fueled by the whale meat, with only short stops to take a drink. That night they slept again, for the few hours the sun spent below the horizon. The next morning Hekja had to force her legs to move. They were so stiff and sore, but there was still more running to do.

Chapter 21

Mist!

The mist came slowly, down from the mountains and up from the sea, till it was thick as barley flour around them and impossible to see the ground.

Hekja slowed, till she realized that the mist made little difference to Snarf. She couldn't see, but he could smell, and this was quite enough for them to find their way.

Suddenly Snarf stopped and sniffed the air. The mist clung to his fur, tiny jewels like the stones in Freydis's brooches. "Gruff," he snorted.

Hekja bent down. "What is it, boy?"

Snarf gave a short yip and this time Hekja heard it too.

"Help!"

Snarf barked again, more loudly this time. Whoever had cried out must have heard him, because he called out louder now. "Please! Help me! Please!"

Hekja looked around in the fog, but there was nothing to see but white. She laid her hand on

Snarf's head and signaled to him to be quiet, so she could listen more closely.

Girl and dog stood motionless. All that could be heard was the sound of their breathing in the quiet air, and then the rustle of a bird. And then it came again.

"Help! Please!"

"Hikki," breathed Hekja.

"Arf," said Snarf, pleased that Hekja had finally worked out what his sense of smell had known all along. He looked at Hekja, waiting for her order. Keep running, or find the man?

But Hekja didn't hesitate. "Find, boy, find," she said.

Snarf bounded into the mist and disappeared. Hekja tried to follow him, then stopped, confused. "Snarf!" she called.

"Arf!"

Hekja followed the sound through the mist. Suddenly she saw something, a different color from the mist and grass and rock: Hikki lying twisted at the bottom of a cliff.

Snarf barked again, as though to say, "Look, he's over there."

"My foot! It's caught!" cried Hikki.

Hekja ran toward him. It was obvious what had happened. Hikki had missed his step in the mist. As he slithered down the cliff face, the rocks had crumbled under him as he fell, trapping his leg.

Hekja knelt down and examined the rock fall, then pushed at the rock above his ankle. Hikki grunted in pain and shook his head. "I've tried," he said. "It's caught fast. Maybe a lever—a bit of wood to prize it off. Otherwise you'll need to go get help."

Hekja could hear uncertainty in his voice. Would Greenlanders venture out in the mist to help a thrall? In Norway Hikki had been the king's valued slave, but things were different here.

She looked around. There was a stand of crooked trees growing near a crevice nearby. Hekja pushed at one of the trunks until it snapped at the base, then shoved the branch under the rock.

The rock began to move. It was just a bit at first, so Hekja could shove another rock beneath, then shove again.

This time the rock shifted, just enough for Hikki to draw his foot away. The rock crashed down. But Hikki was already free.

Sweat dripped down his face, even though his skin was blue with cold. He felt his foot and ankle carefully, then held his hand up to Hekja.

"Help me up," he ordered.

"Are you sure?"

Hikki nodded. "It's bruised, that's all. I can move my toes. It will swell tonight, but for now I can keep on going."

Hekja helped him up. He put his weight on his foot gingerly and then more heavily.

"It's sore, but I can run," he said. He looked at Hekja for a moment without expression, then reached down and picked up the sealskin bundle by his side and unwrapped it. There were strips of dried meat and barley bread, made sweet with dried berries, and rich with butter.

"Here." He divided it into three portions—one for him, one for Hekja and the other for Snarf. Snarf gulped his down as the others ate theirs more slowly.

"I didn't think you would get this far," Hikki said at last. "You really are a runner, even though you're a girl."

Hekja smiled. It was obviously the highest compliment he knew. "Thank you," she said, swallowing the last of her barley bread.

"It's not easy running in a new land," added Hikki. "Especially when you don't know your way. It's dark and misty here and you were all alone."

"I wasn't alone," said Hekja as she patted Snarf and rubbed his ears.

"Even so," said Hikki.

Hekja waited for him to set off again, as fast as he could limp with his bruised leg. But instead he took Hekja's hand.

"Thank you," he said. He hesitated. "I would like to say that I would have done the same for you. But I wouldn't have. I would have seized my chance to be the winner and left you here. You have taught me something." He glanced at the sky as though to work out where the sun was, but the mist was still too thick. "Go," he said. "I'll wait here for as long as it takes to roast a hare, before I run again."

Hekja frowned. "Isn't your leg too sore to run?"

He shook his head. "No. I am giving you a chance to win. It surely isn't far to go now. Call it runner's honor. Now run!"

Hekja ran.

She had lost all sense of direction now, but it didn't matter. Snarf seemed to know which way to go, and Hekja trusted him. Soon she realized what he had been following—the scent of smoke, and fainter still, the smell of roasting meat. People! They were nearly there.

Slowly the mist began to lift. They topped a hill and there was the farm below.

There were fields and sheep and goats and thralls cutting the grass for hay with long sweeps of their scythes.

Snarf lifted up his nose to bark, to announce that they'd arrived. But Hekja put a hand on his head.

"Ssh," she whispered. "Not yet." She turned around and walked back down the hill the way they'd come and sat and waited. Soon she heard the thud of footsteps and there was Hikki, loping through the remnants of the fog, not even puffed.

He stopped when he saw her. "What's wrong?" he demanded. "Are you hurt?"

Hekja stood up. She had worked out exactly what

she was going to say. It would have been better as a song, but there wasn't time to make one. "Call it runner's honor, even if our masters never understand," she said formally. "We may be slaves, but we have both run well. Let us end the race together, so no one wins, or else we both do."

Hikki looked at her for a moment, then he nodded.

And so the race ended with the two runners striding down the hill, hand in hand, to deliver the message to Thorstein Eriksson, with Snarf running at their side.

Chapter 22

A Feast and a Challenge

They returned to Brattahlid in Thorstein's boat. He brought his bales of hides to sell to the traders, a keg of mead[23] for the feast and his neighbors, who wished to join the celebrations.

Someone must have seen the ship as it traveled down the coast, as there was a crowd waiting for them at the pier—Freydis and Thorvard, Leif and Erik and their men, Snorri the Skald and the other traders. The news of Freydis's and Leif's bet had spread.

"Well, younger brother?" demanded Freydis, looking from Thorstein to Hikki and to Hekja. "Who won?"

Thorstein shook his head. "Both of them!" he exclaimed. "I have never seen the like! They came running down the hill together, hand in hand."

"Hand in hand!" cried Freydis. "Is this true?"

Hekja lifted her chin. "Yes," she said.

Freydis's eyes narrowed. "I ordered you to win,"

---

[23] honey wine

she said. "Not play handies with my brother's thrall."

"You told me I would be beaten if I lost," said Hekja. "I didn't lose. I promised I would run my best, and so I did."

Beside her Snorri gave a shout of laughter. "She's got you there!" he cried.

Freydis looked from him to Hikki, to Hekja then to Leif. And then she grinned. "So! I get to keep my cow!"

"And I keep mine," agreed Leif. He too was grinning.

Erik clapped Snorri on the back. "Have they given you an idea for a song, skalder boy?"

Snorri smiled as though the idea was ridiculous. He didn't even look at Hekja and Hikki as he shook his head. "I make songs about heroes, not thralls."

"And your heroes are all men," said Freydis.

Snorri nodded, his hand still on Snarf's head, fondling the big dog's ears. "Of course. Heroes like your father, finding a new land, and your brother, sailing to unknown Vinland and returning."

Freydis looked out at the ocean for a moment and was silent. But Erik looked pleased at being called a hero. He slapped Snorri on the back again, so hard he nearly jolted him into the fiord. "By thunder, that was well said, boy," he cried. "Come and see how heroes feast this afternoon, and you can give us your song. And you thralls, too." Erik turned to Hikki and Hekja and tapped them with his stick. "You can come and listen to his chant, in honor of your run."

"Woof," said Snarf, as though he could smell the meat already.

* * *

The feast was held outdoors. Big as Erik's house was, so many people had come from farms up and down the coast that no house could have held them all.

So the sheep had been moved from a field near the farmhouse so that great fires of driftwood could be lit there, with whale oil to keep them burning well. Two giant bears, walrus, and reindeer were roasting, with great stone platters of wheat bread to soak up their juices. The traders had brought the wheat, for none grew in Greenland. It was their gift for the feast.

There were trestles of other food, too—big stone pots of pickled cod tongues and oat cream puddings with onions and sorrel—plants the settlers had brought from Iceland. There were dishes of buttered angelica and rose root, which grew naturally in Greenland. There were fat ducks stuffed with berries and fish stewed with cream; fermented whale liver and fresh whale steaks; barrels of barley beer and mead and big stone jugs of buttermilk that had been cooling in the ice-flecked stream.

Erik's great carved chair had been brought out, as well as benches and rocks covered with sheepskins for people to sit on.

No one noticed as Hekja crept up to pick some scraps from a reindeer carcass. The visitors all carried their own knives to cut the meat, but Hekja didn't have one. She used one of the spare knives on the tables, next to the long spoons for scooping out the marrow from the bones.

She sliced off some scraps and laid them on a slab of bread, then handed a chunk of meat to Snarf. Snorri the Skald glanced at her, but said nothing. He was talking to one of Leif's daughters, with gold and brass at her wrists and throat. She had her grandfather's bright hair and a look of softness in her eyes. That would be from her mother, perhaps, thought Hekja, as there was no softness in Erik. She overheard two women talking and nodding at the couple as they ate their meat.

"It would be a grand match for her. His family has great lands in Norway, so they say."

The other nodded. "Maybe the lad would like to mix his blood with that of heroes!" They laughed together, but Hekja could see that they were half serious.

Hikki was sitting at the back of the crowd with a big hunk of meat on a slab of bread. He raised a hand to Hekja and she slipped across and sat next to him, grateful for a friendly smile.

The noise and crowds and laughter frightened her a little, as did the men who had drunk too much beer. The women kept the men's drinking horns full and, as no horn could be put down or it would fall over, it was easier to drain it in one gulp and then call for more. The field was full of shouting and yelling, and already there had been a fight, with onlookers cheering the men on.

Suddenly she heard a voice that she remembered. She peered through the wool-clad legs. There was the man Finnbogi, watching the fight, tearing at a hunk of meat with one hand, his ale horn in the other.

"Into him!" he laughed as one man threw another over his shoulder, then pounded his face till he cried for it to stop.

Hekja tensed and hid the trembling of her hand in Snarf's fur. She forced herself to look at other things—the fire sparks streaming to the sky, the girls and women splendid in their brightest scarves, wearing their best necklaces, bangles, and brooches. Even Erik's serving thralls had clean aprons on and colored scarves, although theirs were wool, not silk.

All at once Hekja was conscious of her tattered dress. It was so short you could see her knees now, and her bare feet were hard and callused instead of in soft boots.

Suddenly Erik yelled, "Quiet!" He banged his great stick three times on the ground.

The noise hushed. Bright Eyes, his dog, sat up straight, as though to say, "Pay attention to my master!" People moved closer to Erik's chair, forming a circle around it. All that could be heard were hens muttering indignantly and a calf lowing in the distance for its mother, as the people sat in silence.

"We have been honored," cried Erik, "by a visit from our good friends." He gestured to the traders. "May they return to us often, by thunder, with good profit to us all!"

The crowd roared their approval. Erik banged his stick again. "But we have another honor here tonight! Silence for the skald!"

The young man walked into the circle. His sea-stained clothes were gone. In their place were a silken tunic trimmed with fur that looked as soft as snow, and a blue cloak embellished with gems all down the edges. His cloak pin and rings shone in the sunlight, and the handle of his dagger was carved and bejewelled. His yellow hair was tied back with a bronze clip. He held himself proudly. They all do, thought Hekja, half admiring, half resentful, every person in this land, except the thralls. But this youth looked as though from birth he had known that he was heir to great estates.

Even the men who had been fighting were silent now.

The skald lifted his head to the sky for a moment, then began to sing:

> *"A song in praise,*
> *Of heroes I raise,*
> *Of danger and death,*
> *And the ocean's great depth.*

"But one man defied them,
Though they would destroy him,
For courage fills sails,
With more force than the wind."

The great crowd was silent. Hekja stared at the singer. She had heard her father sing, his voice also so true that people sat quiet even after he had finished. She had heard the men sing on the ship to Greenland. But she had never dreamed a voice could carry as much power as this.

Finally the song's echoes died away and the audience roared again, the men lifting their drinking horns to toast the singer. Erik tore off one of his great brooches and thrust it in Snorri's hand, then clapped him on the back. The young man accepted the brooch as his due and fastened it onto his furs.

Leif's daughter sang next, accompanying herself on a small harp held in her hands. Everyone listened politely, but they weren't standing motionless, like they had for Snorri.

There was a pause after that, as people waited to see if anybody else would sing. Suddenly Hekja wondered what would happen if she began to sing. Her voice was better than Leif's daughter. But probably, she thought, singing was something for free men and women, not for thralls. Even if I could, I wouldn't sing for them. If I sang it would be a gift to them. I will give them nothing.

For a moment the words almost shaped themselves into a song. Hekja smiled to herself. If I ever do sing where they can hear me, she thought, that will be my song.

It was growing dark now. Someone poured more oil on the fires, and Erik's stick beat on the ground again. "Silence! Let the skald sing us another song!" His voice was more quavery than it had been earlier. Erik might have been a hero, but he was getting old and the noise was so loud, they hadn't heard his voice.

In a sudden fit of rage, Erik picked up his carved stick and struck one of the thralls, who was bringing more food out to the tables, on the shoulder. "You! Tell them to be quiet!"

The man nodded. "Yes, master." He made his way over to the men. Hekja saw him pull the sleeve of one, to get his attention and then begin his words.

Hekja was never sure what happened then. But suddenly there was a drunken roar across the crowd.

"No one tells Olaf Njalsson to be silent!"

Metal flashed in the firelight. Hekja bit back a scream and stared across the crowd.

Erik's thrall lay on the ground. His neck was severed. The man he'd asked to be quiet stood over his body, a bloodied axe in his hands. It was one of the traders.

Hekja tried to struggle to her feet. Hikki grabbed her hand and forced her back. No one spoke. A band of silence had tightened around the crowd.

"That could have been you or me," whispered Hikki. "Sit still. This is not a time to be noticed!"

Hekja shook her head numbly. She waited for a howl of rage from Erik. She had heard him howl before, across the fields when his best axe was missing or when a thrall was slow to bring him his spear. But now he said nothing, he simply stared across the crowd at the still bleeding body and then at the man with the axe.

Snorri moved swiftly over to the trader. He whispered something urgently. The man shrugged. He bent and wiped the blood off the axe head on the trodden grass. His axe was a grand one, with carving on the handle, and there were carved bracelets about the man's wrists as well.

Snorri put his hand on the man's arm then, but the trader shook him off. "No one tells Olaf Njalsson to be silent!" he muttered again drunkenly.

Snorri gazed at him, then looked at Erik. Then he made his way through the crowd toward Erik.

"I beg your pardon," he said formally to Erik. "My companion misunderstood. I will pay compensation, on his behalf." His hand went to the purse at his waist. "Shall we say thirty ounces of silver?"

Erik stared at the young man. Surely, thought Hekja, he will be angry. The dead thrall had lived in his house, had worked for him. But Erik didn't even glance at the body again.

"The compensation for a slave is only twelve ounces," said Erik.

Snorri laughed. Despite his youth he seemed quite confident beside the older man. "Forty ounces then! Shall we call it extra compensation for a guest's rudeness to a hero!"

Erik clapped him on the back. "Well said, by thunder! Now let a hero make a gift to you as well! What will you have? Name it!" he yelled, lifting his horn in salute to Snorri, then swallowing its contents in one gulp.

Snorri raised his drinking horn in return and drained it down. He looked around the crowd, considering his prize, then laughed. He pointed to Snarf, who was still snuffling for scraps by the fire. "Give me a hero's dog! And every puppy from his get will remind me of my hosts in Greenland!"

"No!" Hekja spoke before she thought. But what did it matter what they did to her? Nothing mattered if they took Snarf. "No!" she yelled. "No!" She leaped to her feet, but Hikki again forced her down. He thrust his hand over her mouth, muffling her words.

"Hush," he hissed, "or it will be your body on the ground next."

But it was as though no one had heard Hekja's outburst. I am invisible, thought Hekja. Who hears a thrall? She struggled against Hikki's grip, but he held her hard.

Across the crowd, Snorri didn't even glance her way. He just continued, as though he hadn't heard her cry. "On second thoughts, what use is a dog to a singer? Will he make my songs for me?"

Snorri smiled and pointed to the harp that Leif's daughter held. "No, lend me that instrument, so I can play it while I am here, and when I'm gone, you can play it to remember a singer who once had the privilege to play in a hero's hall."

Hikki's hand still covered Hekja's mouth. She stared through the sea of skirts and trousers. Had she heard correctly? Was Snarf still hers?

Leif's daughter laughed and blushed as she handed the singer her harp. A mist of tears and anger clouded Hekja's eyes. Why had Snorri changed his mind? Had he heard her cry? Or had he simply thought of another way to compliment Erik's family? Dimly she heard Hikki say, "If I let you go will you be silent?"

Hekja nodded, and he took his hand away from her mouth.

"I'm sorry," he whispered. "But I had to do it. If you had tried to argue, they'd have killed you." His voice dropped even further. "Or worse."

Across the fire, Erik was delighted. "Well said, skalder boy! Sing us another song of heroes then! Daughter! My mug is dry!"

"He doesn't care," whispered Hekja. "He doesn't care about the poor dead man, or me, or Snarf. We don't exist. We're nothing." Suddenly she wanted to run, as fast as she could, and never stop. But if she ran now, the men would notice her and take it as a challenge. And this time one might catch her.

"Why should he care?" said Hikki, and for the first time Hekja heard bitterness instead of pride in his voice. He might be a grand runner, but he was still a thrall.

Hekja got to her feet. For the third time, Hikki pulled her down. "Stop," he hissed. "If you go now, you'll attract attention. Wait till the skald is singing."

"He should sing of the dead thrall," whispered Hekja. "He should make a lament for his death."

"Forty ounces of silver is all the lament he'll get," said Hikki grimly. "Skalds don't sing of thralls."

Freydis went to fetch her father more mead. Across the crowd another thrall, a woman, bent down toward the dead thrall's body. She was crying. But Hikki was right—the skald didn't even glance her way. He smiled at Leif's daughter and stroked the harp strings with his fingertips, as he began to sing:

> *"Stand upon the mountain,*
> *Gaze beyond the sea,*
> *There is a new land calling,*
> *Singing 'come to me.'*
>
> *"Raise the sails, my shipmates,*
> *Fill the barrels well,*
> *I'll sing of the far horizon,*
> *And what to us befell. . . ."*

The song went on and on. Hekja sat silent in the shadows. Now that the crowd was watching the singer, Hikki got up to leave and held his hand out to help Hekja to her feet. Hekja shook her head at him. Just one last song, she thought. After this I'll go.

Hikki sat down next to her again. Snarf wandered over, unaware of his part in anything that had happened, and curled up beside them, his ears pricked.

Another thrall arrived and helped drag out the body. The singer finished, and the last echoes of the harp died away.

"Well sung, by thunder!" roared Erik. His face was flushed, but there were shadows under his eyes. He looked around the crowd. "A song of heroes! Are there any here who will do what I did, and my son? Sail the unknown waves to find new lands beyond the clouds? Found a colony where none have ever been before?"

It was not said as though he expected an answer, except maybe a few "here heres" as people remembered how brave he'd been, before he'd shrunk with age. But suddenly Freydis spoke up.

"I will!" she cried.

People muttered. Someone laughed at the edge of the crowd. Freydis ignored them.

"I challenge every man here!" she cried. "Who will join me? We will sail south, to the lands my brother found. Lands with trees as tall as mountains and salmon that leap like birds. We will explore the land

and make our fortunes! And once we have settled there, our ships will explore even further!"

Suddenly everyone was still. Then someone cried, "Will you take your husband, too?"

Laughter rippled through the crowd.

Freydis turned on them, her eyes flashing. And then she turned to Thorvard. "Well, husband?" she challenged.

Thorvard stared at her, as though considering. And then he grinned. "Well said, wife. I will come. Who will join us?" His voice rose to a bellow.

No one spoke. And then the singer, Snorri the Skald, pushed forward and joined his hand to Thorvard's. "I'll come," he shouted. "What is the use of singing of heroes, if you refuse to be one!"

"My ship will follow them!" someone else cried.

"And mine!"

"And mine!" It was the man called Finnbogi.

"Four ships then!" roared Erik. "Or five? Leif, will you lead a colony to the land you found?"

"I will," said Leif. "And I will take my household with me."

Chapter 23

A Greenland Winter

All about people chattered, and cheered those who'd said that they would join the expedition. Hekja could feel Hikki stunned and silent beside her. Was this the end of Hikki's hopes of a farm and freedom in Greenland, she thought. She whispered, "Will we have to go as well?"

Hikki nodded. "Yes. We are runners. They will need runners to explore this new land."

Hekja bit her lip. "Vinland is even further away, isn't it?" she whispered.

"From what?" asked Hikki.

"From home," said Hekja quietly.

Hikki's eyes were sympathetic in the firelight. "A thrall's home is with his or her owner. It just makes unhappiness to think otherwise."

Hekja was silent for a moment. Then she said, "What is this Vinland place like?"

"I have spoken to Leif's men who were there," said

Hikki. He sounded happier now he could instruct her again. "It is a wonderful place, they say. Rivers thick with salmon, weather so warm the cattle can eat grass right through the winter, and all the grapes that you can eat."

"What are grapes?"

Hikki shrugged. "Berries I think, that they make a drink called wine from. But it is a good place. No ice, no snow." It was as though he was trying to convince himself. "There will be free land there, too. Better land than here." Hekja could see he was remembering Leif's promise to free him and give him land if he worked well.

Hekja gazed up at the mountains. The ice gleamed, even in the starlight. "Why don't they all go to this Vinland then, instead of staying here?"

"Because it is so far away," said Hikki. "And Leif only discovered it three years ago. Maybe they will all follow us in time." He was looking brighter now. "But by then maybe I will have a farm of my own. I will be free. Maybe," he added, "maybe we will both be free."

* * *

Hekja had assumed they would set out at once, but it seemed that it took a long time to plan an expedition like this. Besides, it would be winter soon, and the seas would be too full of ice to sail. Summer was the time to go a-Viking, when the days were long.

The traders sailed away two days after the feast,

with their ivory and walrus-skin ropes, their sealskins and eiderdown. Only Snorri the Skald stayed with Erik and Leif.

Now autumn was half over, it was harvest time. The days of hunting parties were gone. Thorvard had the household up each day as soon as the world brightened, but there was no need to urge the men to work. Thrall, freeman—and husbondi[24]—all would starve together if summer's harvest wasn't stored in time for the bitter Greenland winter.

The cows were left unmilked so that they might put on fat to help keep them alive. Hekja was sent to gathering grass that men cut for hay to feed the animals when the snow lay on the ground. The cut grass was left to dry in the sun, then raked into heaps, then stacked by Erik's man, Arnkel the Strong Hand, who could make a haystack so tight that water flowed off it and the hay inside stayed dry and sweet.

Whale blubber was boiled down for oil; the beaches were scoured for driftwood. Even twigs were bound together and dried for faggots. More fish was smoked or dried. Whale tongues and strips of blubber were preserved to chew in the cold weather.

Then there was the grain to thresh and more grass to cut, and more grass again, till it seemed to Hekja that all of Greenland was either ice or rock or drying haystacks.

Sometimes she heard Snorri sing as he swung his

---

[24] master of the household

scythe, for in this season, even honored visitors had to work in the fields. At times Hekja found she was humming the tunes too. It made her long for music even more. But there was no chance to sing her own songs with everyone else around.

Snarf enjoyed the grass cutting. The mice had bred up as the grain ripened, and the scythes sent them scurrying. He could catch a bellyful on a good day. But the best was still to come, from a dog's point of view, for it was time to slaughter the livestock. The bull calves, lambs, the oldest of the cows and sheep, and most of the hens and pigs would go. There was no way to store enough grain and hay to feed them all.

So their necks were slit and the hot blood was collected and mixed with oats and herbs to make blood puddings. Then it was stuffed into lengths of intestines that had been washed clean in the streams. They were then hung to dry up in the rafters, while Snarf watched and drooled and begged for leftovers.

Calves' stomach was kept for rennet, to turn milk into curds, then cheese, the legs and back strips smoked and salted and hung to dry above the fire, the head boiled down for brawn, the fat boiled to a hard, white lard and the lean meat cut into thin strips and hung to dry. Fish was either gutted or kept with their roes. You could hardly see the houses for the lines of drying food.

All through summer the crocks of butter had been

buried in the cool soil by the stream, and every second day a new cheese hung up in the dairy. Now the eggs were buttered too and stored in straw. The onions were hung up in the storerooms, with their stems plaited. Below them were the watercress, angelica stems, rose root leaves, and casks of sorrel dried into whispery flakes.

Then one morning Hekja woke and found the world outside was silent.

She tiptoed over to the big wood doors and peered outside. Everything was white. Even the air was white. Snow was still falling, muffling every sound.

Someone stepped up behind her. It was Thorvard. He took one look outside, then yelled, "Blizzard! Hurry! We have to get the animals inside!"

Inside the men groaned, then scrabbled for their cloaks. But Freydis called Hekja back.

"Here." She thrust some sealskin boots at her. They were lined with fur and matched a long calfskin cloak in Freydis's hand. It was not much of a cloak—the hide was barely trimmed—but it was warmer than the one she had. "Thank you, mistress," said Hekja.

Freydis shrugged. "If you lose your toes to frostbite, you cannot work," she said. She nodded at the boots. "Mind you dry those out before you put them on, or your toes will freeze. We keep no crippled slaves in this household."

Hekja didn't ask what happened to a crippled slave. She slipped the boots over her feet, fastened the cords of the cloak, and ran outside after the others. Her toes took a moment to get used to the clumsiness of boots.

It was so bright in the daylight that her eyes hurt. Hekja helped the men drive the cattle into their byres. The poor things were shivering, and glad to escape the snow. The pigs had already found their way into the pig shed. The sheep were driven into the house. They would live at one end and the humans at the other, to help keep each other warm.

That first snow melted by the afternoon, and there was no more for days after that, so the last of the hay dried out and was brought in. But the next snow lay upon the ground and the one after, too, and then it was just constant days of more snow and ice. The snow piled up so high about the house that the men spent most days just digging out the door and tramping the snow flat to make a walkway to the byres and sheds, so that Hekja and Gudrun could feed the animals their winter rations of hay and grain.

The household woke in darkness now, till Freydis lit the fish-oil lamp, but only one, as the oil had to last till summer came. By early afternoon it was dark again. They lived in shadows, for even when it was light outside, there was little light indoors. It was a darkness that dragged at you and made you long for summer.

The men sat by the fire and played chess or told stories of storms at sea or plundering villages. Even as they played or talked their hands were busy, carving wood or walrus ivory into spoons, or runners for the sleighs, needles, or jewelry.

The women worked too. Hekja mostly spent her days combing wool for Gudrun to spin into thread on her spindle, while Freydis sat up on the weaving platform with the loom, weaving the cloth for the household or for sails. Sometimes Gudrun sewed trousers or made dresses and aprons. She tried to teach Hekja how to use a sewing needle too. Hekja wasn't very good, but she kept working at it, as one of the woolen dresses was for her, with a proper head-dress, too. She had almost outgrown the dress she had worn since her capture.

Sometimes Hekja combed Snarf with the wool comb, which made Gudrun laugh and threaten to spin his long hair into thread.

* * *

Midwinter brought the Yule feast. "And it's a grand one, hey?" said Gudrun happily. "A whole week long, our household and Master Leif's and Master Erik's!"

"And barley beer enough for everyone, and a bull calf kept to roast," said Conlan the Irish thrall long-ingly, from his place by the fire. "If I eat another fish, I will turn into one and go swimming down the fiord with the mermaids."

Hekja looked up from the spindle she was twirling. "Do thralls go to the feast as well?"

Conlan nodded. "We do indeed. And we can eat

and drink as much as we want to, with singing and games, too."

By Yule morning the snow had formed a crust, and Hekja's feet left deep holes as she padded out to see to the animals. Even though the sun had risen low on the horizon the day was dim, as though the darkness had crushed all brightness from the air.

There was the scent of roasting meat from Erik's farm across the fields. Hekja felt like dancing through the snow! It had been so long since she had left the house, apart from brief visits across the yard, so long since she had seen a person who was not from her household. And there would be fresh meat from the rare winter hunts and feasting food, instead of hard dried fish and gruelk from ground fish bones. And music too . . .

Freydis stepped out from her and Thorvard's curtained room as Hekja took off her wet boots. Freydis had on her best cloak, and all her jewelry. Thorvard wore his best furs. Freydis picked up her cloak, then glanced at Hekja, who was putting on some dry boots—she had worn Gudrun's spare pair to keep her new ones dry.

"Not you," said Freydis shortly.

Hekja looked up. "Mistress?" she inquired.

"Someone must stay and keep the fire alight and tend to the animals."

Hekja took the boots off again and came back to the fire pit. She felt the disappointment like a blow.

Gudrun patted her hand. "It will be your turn to go to the feast next year, perhaps," she said.

"Next year," said Freydis, "we will be in the new land."

Chapter 24

Yule Feast

They left her then.

"Eat what you want from the storeroom," were Freydis's parting words. "It is Yuletide, after all. You may keep a lamp alight, and the fire, but use no more wood or oil than you must. Feed the beasts and give them fresh hay, but don't bother to muck them out—the men can do that when we return. A week of dung will do no harm."

The door closed behind them. Hekja could hear them chattering as they slid on the fresh snow. Thorvard laughed, as he picked his wife up in his arms to keep her feet dry.

At least they had left Snarf, Hekja thought. She felt guilty at that, for she knew Snarf would have enjoyed the excitement of the feast. But without Snarf she would be quite alone, except for the sheep. And sheep, thought Hekja, were even stupider companions than cows.

It was quiet, after they had left. No, not really

quiet, she thought. The sheep bleated. The wind came up again and howled, though the sod roof kept it out. The fire flickered and a mouse rustled in the moss, chinking between the stones. Snarf snuffled after it, then put his nose on his paws and dozed by the fire, with one ear pricked to make sure the sheep didn't push past the hurdle that kept them in their part of the house.

Hekja sat by the fire and twirled her spindle. There was nothing else to do now the animals had been fed, except go to the storeroom of the main hall to fetch fish for supper. There were dried berries in a basket, and she took a handful of those, too. After all, Freydis had told her to eat what she liked. It was little enough for a Yule feast, thought Hekja as she chewed the hard, tough berries.

The day passed slowly. Hekja felt its gloom sweep through her. Winters were so long and dark in Greenland, far longer than at home. At least she'd had the feast to look forward to. Now there were just more dark dull days—the tomorrows seemed endless.

Finally she went to sleep with Snarf and the sheep for company. It seemed so much darker and colder, Hekja thought, without other people near.

There was no snowfall during the night, so the doorways were still clear in the dimness next morning. Hekja fed the cattle crammed up in their stalls and carried in fresh hay for the sheep, while Snarf lifted his leg on the doorposts. But today, despite the cold, Hekja hesitated before going back indoors. The hill looked so inviting, white and pure despite the darkness of the day. She could run up there, just for a while, into the peace and freshness, just her and Snarf like they used to do. . . .

"Arf," said Snarf encouragingly. He leaped up and licked her face. "Arf arf!"

Hekja shook her head. It wasn't worth the risk. She had seen how worthless thralls were. She had been told to guard the house and keep the fire alight. If she left without permission, Thorvard or Freydis could kill her and no one would even question what they'd done.

It would be easy to escape, now everyone was gone. But where to? Only into the snow and ice and dark, where they would surely die.

Hekja went indoors again, and sat down by the fire. But this time she didn't pick up her spindle. Why bother with the boring work when there was no one to order her around? At least she could spend this time as she liked.

She would sing. But not an old song, not one of Pa's. They belonged to the past. No, she'd sing a new song, for herself and Snarf. She reached out for the words, and then the tune came too.

"Snow on the hillside,
Mountain and sky,
The whole world shivers,
As winter flows by.

"Empty and longing,
Lonely as I,
The wind howls as it searches,
For . . ."

"Hoooooooowwwwwwl!"

It was impossible to tell if Snarf was joining in, or complaining about the noise. Hekja broke off singing. She laughed and hugged him. The mouse rustled again, and Snarf darted after it. Hekja began to sing again.

The door opened.

"Who is that?" demanded Snorri the Skald. "Who is singing?" He was dressed in furs, a fur hood and fur-trimmed boots and mittens, and there were flakes of snow on his face.

Hekja stood up respectfully. "No one, Master Skald," she said. "My dog was howling, that was all."

"Arf," welcomed Snarf, his mouth full of mouse. He swallowed it. "Arf arf."

"It didn't sound like a dog," said Snorri. He stepped inside. The sheep moved restlessly as they watched the newcomer. The snow was melting on Snorri's face, and he wiped it off.

"Maybe it was the wind," offered Hekja. She picked up the spindle and began to twirl it.

Snorri looked at her curiously. "Perhaps. Or maybe the ice giants were calling, up in the mountains."

"Are there really ice giants?" asked Hekja cautiously. Gudrun had told her there were, but she had never quite believed it.

Snorri smiled. "Not that anyone has ever met. Not anyone sober, at any rate. Or maybe they have, and haven't lived to tell the tale."

He walked down the hall, then sat down in Thorvard's chair, and looked around the house. "There is a legend that poetry was stolen from the dwarfs," he added. "Maybe the dwarfs sing in this land, in winter when the people are indoors."

"I wouldn't know," said Hekja. She looked down at her spindle as though it was the most fascinating thing in the world. "I have only been here since past midsummer."

"Where are you from?"

Hekja shrugged. "I don't know the name your people give to my island. No one bothered to tell me," she added bitterly. "They simply came and killed and left." She lifted her chin. "Perhaps you would like to make a chant of that? A tale of heroes, fighting girls and women and men who have no swords."

For a moment Snorri looked shocked. Then he looked angry. Suddenly Hekja realized what she had done. It was the song, she thought. I forgot I was a thrall when I was singing. Now she was here alone with a Norseman, one that she had angered and insulted.

Could she reach the door before he grabbed her? Then the anger left his face.

"You don't understand," he said gruffly.

155

Hekja nodded. "No. That is true." She spoke respectfully, and hoped he didn't sense what lay underneath.

"All men fight," said Snorri, "it is what men do. And the best men win. How can a man test his courage except in battle? And the brave deserve their reward."

And what of those who lose, thought Hekja, or who never wanted to fight at all? But she kept twirling her spindle. Snarf sniffed Snorri's feet, then lay down again at Hekja's side.

"Tell me truthfully," said Snorri, now in a gentler voice. "Was it you singing?"

"Yes," said Hekja. There was no point denying it now.

Snorri shook his head. "What is your mistress thinking of?" he cried. "She should have brought you to the feast! A voice like yours would drive the dark away!" He stood up and made his way back to the door. "And I'll tell her so at once," he added. "Yule isn't a time to spend alone."

"Please . . ." Hekja ran to the door and called after him.

He turned. "What is it?"

"Please . . . please don't tell them I can sing."

Snorri stared. "Why ever not?"

Would he understand? Or would she anger him again?

"Because . . . because a slave has nothing. No belongings, no past that anybody cares to know, no future unless her mistress gives her one. My songs are all I have. If you tell them, they will own those, too."

Snorri stared at her as though he had never seen a thrall before. Then he turned and stamped through the watching sheep and out the door. Hejka watched him trudge across the snow through the endless twilight toward the feast.

Would he tell Freydis to punish her? She couldn't tell.

Hekja went back to the fire and stirred it up so the sparks rose in the smoky air. The wind was rising; it muttered down the smoke hole, sending a gust of snowflakes through the house. Hekja threw on more wood—the updraft of a good fire kept even a blizzard out.

Suddenly the door opened again. It was one of Erik's thralls, an old woman, with almost as good a beard as Erik. "Your mistress says you are to go to the feast," she said. "I will stay here in your stead."

Hekja stared. "When did she say this?"

"Just now." The old woman smiled. "Off you go, girl. It will do me good to have a rest, away from all the noise. I will mind the house and animals."

"Did the mistress say anything else?" asked Hekja. "About singing, maybe?"

The woman shook her head. "Nothing else."

Hekja pulled on her boots and fastened her cloak. Snarf bounded out after her, and they set off across the snow.

Light gleamed through the doors of Erik's farmhouse. There must be dozens of lamps burning, thought Hekja, driving away the winter dark. She could hear men's voices singing, and the scent of bread and roasting meat filled the air that the heavy snow had left odorless.

Freydis was sitting just inside the door, a mug of mead in her hand. She nodded to Hekja. "The young poet there suggested someone else take your place." Freydis sounded amused. "I should have thought of it myself," she added. "Old Sigrun is more than happy to snooze Yule away by a fire."

Gudrun smiled at Hekja from the seats by the fire pit, and Hikki moved over to give her space on his bench. Hekja glanced at Snorri, but he didn't even glance her way—he was too enthralled by Leif's tale of a farmhouse that had been crushed by a glacier, killing all inside. He even ignored Snarf when he sniffed hopefully at the pouch where he had once kept dried meat.

So Snarf went to sniff Bright Eyes instead, and for once she didn't growl at him to go away.

It was a grand Yule feast. There were games with the other thralls, and music from the skald and Leif's daughter, and stories from Erik in his great chair. Once Leif spoke of Vinland, its giant trees and lush grass, and Freydis's gaze burned as bright as the fire. And then the week was over, and no one had mentioned Hekja's singing at all.

Chapter 25

A Hero's Farewell

Erik the Red died toward the end of winter. Many people died at winter's end, from poor food or not enough, and from the bitter cold. But Erik died from none of those. He was in his chair, playing chess, pondering his next move, just as he had pondered settling a new land twenty years before. And then he gave a cry, toppled from his chair, and died.

Freydis was weaving, and Hekja and Gudrun were spinning when the thrall came running with the news. "Mistress," he panted, as Freydis looked up from her loom. "His lordship . . . his Lordship's dead!"

There was no doubt which Lordship he meant— The Lordship always referred to Erik. Freydis stood up, her face expressionless. Thorvard had been carving a new runner for the sleigh. He stood too and looked as though he might make a move to comfort her. But she shook her head at him.

"Come," she said shortly. "We will help with the

funeral." She reached for her cloak and gestured to the men to come as well.

It took both households three days' work to prepare Erik's grave. He was a Christian—his wife had built the first church in Greenland—but it was fitting that he be buried as a Viking hero, too.

Hekja and Hikki were sent to run to every household within a day's journey, to let them know of Erik's death. The seas were too frozen to send out ships.

This time both ran together—running in winter was dangerous, and both carried ropes in case the other fell into a fissure in the snow. If it had been summer the whole colony might have been invited to the funeral, but this was not possible in blizzard season.

It was strange running in the winter silence. Even the trees and rocks were white. The ice mountains gleamed in the sunlight. The glaciers rumbled as they carved their way out to the sea.

The husbondi of the last farmhouse they reached offered them a place in his sleigh, so Hekja was back at Brattahlid for the funeral.

The thralls had dug a giant pit, and Erik's ship was lowered into it. His grave goods were piled around—his sword and shield, the carved chair he had sat in since his house was built, his sleigh and snowshoes, even his sleeping furs.

Snorri carved a funeral poem in runes in the shape of a snake onto a stone. No one told Hekja what they said, but she imagined that they spoke of heroes.

There was some talk of killing a female thrall as well, to keep him company in the afterworld. Hekja's face whitened when she overheard this, but nothing came of it—not because a thrall was valued, but because it was a pagan custom and too many disapproved.

Finally, as women wailed, Erik's final ship was covered by a mound of dirt, outlined with big stones, and a cross put at the head.

Freydis stood silent as the frozen dirt was shoveled back into the pit. Even when Thorvard tried to comfort her, she shook him off and went to stand alone on the hillside, staring down at her father's grave.

What was she thinking, Hekja wondered. Of songs and games when she was young? Of how her father hadn't lived long enough to see his daughter claim a country too?

It was impossible to tell.

Finally the echoes of the last song had died away, and the mourners left the graveside.

Erik the hero, discoverer of Greenland, founder of the colony, fighter and chief, was gone.

* * *

It was fully dark when Hekja heard the noise outside. The lamp had flickered down, and the hall was quiet. At first she thought the men were singing another lament for Erik. But this sound was different.

Hekja made her way across the hall and passed the

restless sheep as quietly as she could, then looked outside. The night was lighter than indoors, for the full moon cast shadows on the snow.

The noise came again. "Hoooooowwwwwwwwwwwl!"

Hekja peered across the fields to Erik's grave. Bright Eyes and Snarf sat on the great mound. As Hekja watched, they lifted up their heads again and howled for the dead master.

The sound floated past the farms, over the fiords, up to the mountains of ice and snow, across the glaciers, above this cold and foreign land that Erik had made his own. The dogs sang their own song, one that had no need for human words. A song to honor a hero, in the best way they knew how.

The rest of the household was still asleep when Snarf slipped indoors. When Hekja cuddled him, his fur felt like ice, and so did his nose. She hoped that Bright Eyes had found someone to give her comfort too.

Chapter 26

After the Funeral

Freydis was rich now. Erik's big house and the main fields would go to Leif. Freydis inherited two smaller farms, with the allegiance of the men who worked them, as well as the farm Erik had given her on her marriage. Erik's wealth of silver was divided among Leif, Thorvard, and Freydis.

Hekja watched Freydis at her weaving the day after the funeral. Freydis had never shed a tear since the news had come of Erik's death, not that Hekja had seen.

Freydis's face was still expressionless. She said nothing all morning until it was time to order Gudrun to serve the meal—fish stewed in water and thickened with reindeer moss, for now at winter's end all of the meat was gone. The household was spooning up the tasteless stew from the big pot when Leif bent his head under the door lintel. No Norse door was ever tall enough to walk through with one's head held high—it was easier to slice off an enemy's head if he had to duck to come in the door.

But today Leif was no enemy. He took off his cloak, shook off the snowflakes, and came in to stand by the fire.

Freydis didn't offer him fish—Erik's, or rather Leif's, household had many times as many thralls and beasts as hers, and was better supplied. While her household ate dried fish, Leif's still dined on meat.

"What is it?" Freydis asked her brother shortly.

Leif took a breath. "The Vinland expedition—it is impossible now. We must send runners to the other households to let them know."

Freydis didn't even look up from her fish. "Why?"

Leif stared. "Surely you must see that! I must take Father's responsibilities here. I can't go wandering off beyond the horizon."

"Why not?" said Freydis cooly. "That is what Father did."

"Father was outlawed for three years and had his lands forfeited for unlawful killing. He had no choice but to leave Iceland. I have my duty here."

Freydis put her bowl aside. "Then we will go without you."

Leif stared at her. "A woman, lead an expedition?"

"Why not?"

"You know why not! How will you get men to follow a woman? You have never been to Vinland! How will you even find it?"

Freydis laughed. "You forget, brother. You've been

boasting of your voyage for two years! You gave the poet every detail, so many days to the south, so many to the west. In fact, I am sure we can do better than you, and sail straight to Vinland, without your troublesome adventures on the way."

"Freydis . . ." Leif looked at Thorvard. "You are her husband! Say something! Tell her it's impossible."

Freydis didn't give her husband time to reply. "The ship is mine," she said shortly. "And the farm men are mine as well. Whether my husband chooses to come or not, I am going."

"I am coming," said Thorvard, just a bit too softly. He held Leif's eyes as though in challenge.

Freydis's gaze was triumphant. "We shall see how many choose to follow Erik's daughter, instead of staying moldering at home with his son."

"But . . ." began Leif. He stopped and shook his head. "There is no arguing with you. A proper wife would . . ." He stopped at the expression on Thorvard's face.

Thorvard's fingers inched toward his axe. "You may be her brother, Leif Eriksson, but I will have no man insult my wife and live."

Leif turned on his heel, grabbed his cloak, and left.

Chapter 27

Freydis's Followers

It seemed to Hekja that one day they lived in twilight, then all of a sudden the days were so bright they hardly needed the lamps at all. Gudrun laughed at her surprise. "It's the ice giants," she explained. "They sit up in the ice mountains and watch the winter sun. They are so big, they hide it from everybody else. But as soon as the sun begins to rise higher in the sky for spring, they sit down again. And bump! The days are longer, hey?"

Hekja longed for spring to come properly. By now the salt fish was so hard, it needed soaking for three days. Most of the household had coughs from months of breathing smoke and fish-oil fumes, and her voice was hoarse as well. The house and every person in it stank of sweat, sheep, and fish.

The snow melted in the warmer days, dripping down the smoke hole, then freezing again into icicles overnight. More snow fell; this time it looked like silvery puffs that the fresh sunlight turned to magic.

Finally the patches of mud among the drifts of snow turned green, then the green all turned to flowers. Butterflies hovered just out of reach when Snarf tried to snap them. His fur was falling out in big, thick handfuls, and finally Gudrun made good her threat to spin some into thread. It looked quite fine, but smelled so much like wet dog that Freydis refused to weave it.

Thorvard and the thralls carried the cattle out onto the green grass—the cows were too weak to stand by now, much less walk, for there had been little hay and no grain at all for the last month of winter. After the first reindeer hunt, there was fresh meat, even though it was winter tough and stringy with not a speck of fat. There was fresh fish to eat as well. The hens were well fed on fish guts and reindeer heart and soon began to lay eggs. A whale was sighted out past the fiord, too, so even if there was no grain or milk or cheese, there was more whale meat than anybody wanted. Hekja could no longer feel Snarf's ribs through his fur, or her own underneath her dress.

She was glad of the good food, for now that the snows had partly cleared, Freydis sent Hekja on a mission. She was to run to the farms of the men who had promised to join Freydis's expedition, to tell them of her plans. Freydis wanted details of what men and ships they each would bring.

But each time, Hekja came back with a refusal.

Freydis took each message calmly, though her face grew stonier than before. Without Leif's leadership, the men had changed their minds.

Hekja was sent to Finnbogi's farm last, as it was further away than the others, up north where the snows kept their grip for longer. He and his brother relied more on hunting seals than on farming. In fact, Finnbogi had accompanied Leif on the voyage to sell his sealskins when Hekja had been taken.

It took Hekja four days to run to Finnbogi's. Each night when she stopped to rest she saw him in her dreams, his face above her mother, his laughter and the blood. Finnbogi had made no sign he ever remembered chasing Hekja or killing her mother. Hekja was just another thrall now, among so many. At least she hoped so.

Finally Hekja came to the fiord with the black rock slope and the glacier above it. It was white and cold, just as Thorvard had described. There was the farm, too, a big main house with a few thin cows and long lines where sealskins flapped in the wind. Down below Finnbogi's ship rode the milky fiord water. Even this early in the season, it was evident they had been fishing or sailing north to seal. Whatever else Finnbogi was, it was evident he was an excellent seaman.

A young thrall opened the door. She was no older than Hekja, but thinner faced. It seemed Finnbogi's household didn't eat as well in the winter months as Freydis's. She stared at Hekja in astonishment.

"Who are you?" she cried.

"I am Freydis's runner," said Hekja, as calmly as she could. She kept wondering every moment if Finnbogi would appear. "I come with a message for your master."

Another thrall came to the door. She was a few years older than the first, but still young. Hekja swallowed her contempt. She had learned enough from Freydis to know that older, experienced thralls were more valuable in a good household. It seemed that Finnbogi's thralls weren't chosen for their skill at making cheese. The young thrall also stared at Hekja, as though she had never seen a female runner.

Now another woman pushed the thrall away. She was middle-aged, with thin gray hair plastered to her scalp, a sharp face, and narrow lips. This must be Finnbogi's wife, Hekja realized, the mistress of the house, though she wore none of the fine brooches or bracelets of the other Viking mistresses.

Hekja gave her message again. Finnbogi's wife shrugged her bony shoulders. "He is in the fletching shed.[25] Gunnhild! Go fetch the master!"

Hekja waited for the woman to ask her in and offer food and drink. But she just stood there staring, till Hekja heard Finnbogi's footsteps from the shed.

Finnbogi's hands were bloody. It is just seal blood from the fletching shed, Hekja told herself. But she still shivered.

---

[25] This was where the skins were fletched, i.e., cleaned and tanned.

"Well?" demanded Finnbogi abruptly.

"My mistress Freydis has sent a message," recited Hekja, as she had so many other times. "She intends to sail when the first crops are sown, after the next new moon. She wants to know if you will still join her."

"Why not?" asked Finnbogi cooly. "I have sailed with Leif before."

Hekja flushed. "Master Leif will not be going. Master Erik died this winter, and Master Leif must look after the farms. But he has said his sister can use the longhouses he built in Vinland, and he gives all his claim to the land to her."

Finnbogi gave a bark of laughter. "I see! And I bet none of the others will follow a woman. Neither will I!"

Hekja felt relief course through her. She hated to bring more bad news to Freydis, but at least she need never see this man again. She bent her head politely. "I will tell my mistress . . ." she began.

"Not so fast . . . Tell her I will come as her partner. We each bring thirty men, no more. All profit will be split equally, half for her, half for me. Go tell your mistress that and come back if she agrees."

He turned his back on her and walked back to the fletching shed. Hekja waited a moment in case his wife invited her in to rest and have a meal, as every other household had done.

But his wife just stared at Finnbogi's departing

back. "There had better be a good profit," she muttered to herself. "Better than a life of seal porridge and whale blubber." She turned her back and slammed the door.

Hekja jogged out of the courtyard, trying to ignore her hunger. She had eaten all the food Gudrun had packed her, but at least she hadn't had to linger at Finnbogi's.

The scream of a bird made her look up. Hekja grinned to herself as she clambered carefully down the fiord cliffs. It was spring! She knew where there'd be food to find now.

Sure enough, there were gulls' eggs on the first ledge she found. Hekja gathered them in her skirt and climbed away from the furious parent birds before she sucked one from the shell. Had it only been a year ago she had eaten eggs at home? Homesickness bit deeper suddenly. Freydis could wait just a little longer for her answer, she decided.

She made a driftwood fire, lighting it with the iron and flint she carried with her these days, far enough from Finnbogi's so no one would see the smoke. She baked the rest of the eggs in the coals. She wished Snarf was with her, to eat them too, just as he had before. But Snarf was hunting with Thorvard.

Hekja peeled the eggs one by one and nibbled them as she gazed out to sea. Home was there, across the water. Or was it? What was left of everything she knew? Perhaps even the girls were gone, to husbands further up the coast, the cows serving as their dowries, or even to other islands. Maybe even Tikka's hut was empty.

Hekja shut her eyes and let Ma's face float before her. But when she tried to think of Bran, Snorri's face was there instead.

Hekja opened her eyes, annoyed. Snorri had a golden voice and his songs were . . . good, Hekja admitted. But that was no reason for him to slide into her dreams. Besides, it was time for her to get going.

Freydis stood silently as Hekja repeated Finnbogi's message. Then she said abruptly, "Go and eat, and sleep. Hikki can take my message back."

"Please, mistress," said Hekja. "What will the message be?"

For a moment Hekja thought Freydis might rebuke her. But then she said, "Hikki can tell him yes. Tell Finnbogi I agree."

Chapter 28

Leaving Greenland

It had been arranged that Finnbogi and his brother would set sail from their farm, the day after the full moon. They would meet Freydis at Brattahlid, and both ships would sail on from there.

Full moon came and went and the moon grew thin again. But there was no sign of Finnbogi. Finally Freydis ordered that the ship be loaded. They would wait for old Thrand Egilsson—the most experienced sailor in the Brattahlid district—to declare the weather would hold for the next few days. Then they would sail, whether Finnbogi came or not.

There was nothing for Hekja to pack. She had the dress she wore, her rags from home, her boots, her cloak, and that was all. But the morning they were to leave, Freydis beckoned from her curtained room at the end of the longhouse. She handed Hekja a pile of clothing. "Here," she said.

"Should I put them in your packs?" asked Hekja, thinking that Freydis wanted her to store them in the waterproof sealskins for her.

"No, they're for you. Two dresses," said Freydis. "New ones. There's no point giving you old dresses of mine—I'm twice your size. There are aprons, too, and boots, and another cloak." She handed Hekja another bundle, smaller than the first. "This is for you, too. It's a tunic like the one Hikki wears, when he runs. People would have been shocked if you wore it here. But in Vinland it will be useful when you are scouting out the land."

"Thank you," said Hekja.

Freydis hesitated. "The other women coming with us are not thralls," she added. "But you'll be passing on my orders to them. It will be easier for you to have authority if you're dressed well. I'd also like you to have these."

Freydis handed Hekja a hairbrush. It was backed with walrus ivory and carefully carved. Hekja's eyes widened at its beauty. Then Freydis undid one of the brooches on her apron. Hekja stared. The brooch was gold.

"For me?"

Freydis nodded. "Partly because a brooch like this indicates your status. But also . . ." Again Freydis hesitated. "Because I trust you," she said at last. "And I think in this new land I will need someone I can trust. Someone who'll do what I say unconditionally, even though I'm a woman." Freydis paused again, as though trying to find the words. "We are founding a new land in Vinland. Always with new lands, there are more men than women, at least at first. There'll come a time when a man asks to buy you from me, so you can be freed to marry. But a runner can't run when she's pregnant. I ask that you do not commit to any man for three years. After that, you will be free."

Hekja looked at the ground, and then at Freydis. "What if I don't want a husband?"

Freydis blinked at that. "Why ever not?" She smiled one of her rare true smiles. "It's what free women do."

"Some might say that women don't lead expeditions," said Hekja. "I . . . I saw what Norsemen do to women in my village. I want none of that."

"Ah," said Freydis quietly. And then she said, "It is not always like that with men and women. Do you think I would put up with a man who treated me like that?"

Hekja shook her head. "No."

"You'll have many offers down in Vinland. Do well by me, and I'll make sure you have silver or cows or land enough to take to your marriage to ensure respect."

"But if I don't want a husband?" persisted Hekja. "Can I still be free?"

"Free to do what?" Freydis was genuinely perplexed.

Hekja was silent—thinking of her home. Then she said, "Just be free."

Freydis thought awhile. It was clear she had never

thought what a freed woman thrall might do, except to marry. "Very well," Freydis said at last. "If you marry, I'll give you land and cows or silver. If you do not, you can have them anyway. But I expect good service and total loyalty." She walked swiftly from the room without waiting for a reply.

So on her last day in Greenland, Hekja was finally dressed like a true Greenland woman. She left the house, in her new wool dress and boots, her apron and her scarf, and the gold brooch. She had grown in the past year, but still only came to Freydis's shoulder. She would never truly look like she belonged, not with her dark hair and eyes.

It was hard for Hekja to say good-bye to Gudrun. Gudrun was too old and crippled to be of use in Vinland, but she had given Hekja more kindness than anyone since she had left her own village.

"Take care, dear girl," whispered Gudrun as Hekja hugged her in the doorway. "Watch out for those fierce unipeds."[26]

Hekja left Gudrun gazing from the doorway as she followed the men down to the waiting ship by the pier. It was a large ship, but it looked so small to be venturing out onto the wide sea.

The towboats were already loaded, with sacks of seed and tools, but the animals had to come in the big ship, as they would need water during the voyage and quieting when things got rough.

---

[26] one-legged mythical monsters believed to live in the south

176

Most of the folk of Brattahlid had come to see them off. Leif's daughter was there, talking earnestly with Snorri the Skald. Hekja wondered if she was coming too, but Snorri boarded the ship alone. He hardly glanced at Hekja, even in her new dress, and when he did it was as though he deliberately forced his glance away.

When Leif arrived, Hekja and Snarf were still standing with Freydis and Thorvard on the hill above the pier. He was alone, except for Erik's dog, Bright Eyes, who kept close to Leif's side now.

The dogs sniffed each other, exchanging news. Bright Eyes had had a litter of pups in early spring, and Hekja wondered if they were Snarf's. Suddenly she saw Hikki coming down the hill, his rolled sleeping bag and cloak in his arms. She hadn't been able to speak to him since Yule, but no one had told her that any of Leif's household were coming to Vinland too.

It seemed that even if Leif were not coming, his runner was, a gift from Leif the Lucky.

"Thank you," Freydis was saying to her brother.

Leif nodded. "I will keep an eye on your farms of course," he said.

"So you have promised," said Freydis cooly. Brother and sister looked at each other for a moment. Then Freydis said, "Try to understand. You spent your youth a-Viking. Am I to be suffocated in the house and cheese room, with nothing but my loom to occupy me?"

"It is what women do," said Leif uncomfortably.

Freydis smiled. "Our father was outcast from Norway and from Iceland for doing what he wanted, not what people thought he should. We are both his children."

Leif said nothing. He just hugged her roughly and slapped Thorvard on the back. Then he marched back up the hill, without staying to watch them leave.

Suddenly Snarf stared at the boat, as though he had just realized Hekja expected him to get on board, and live on fish again instead of meat.

"Arf," he said unwillingly. But he followed her as she walked across the plank and felt the rocking of the ship again under her feet.

There were three other dogs on board. Snarf ignored them. This was his second summer and he had reached his full great height, taller than any other dog around.

Hekja had thought the ship she had arrived in was crowded, but here every inch was crammed. The ship rode low in the water. She wedged herself onto a sack of oats next to Hikki and made room for Snarf. "I didn't know you were coming!" she said. "Did you ask to come?"

Hikki shook his head. "I didn't know myself till this morning. I think Leif had only just decided."

"Do you mind?" Hikki shook his head again. He seemed preoccupied.

"There are more than thirty men on board," he said.

Hekja looked around. She could count now, but had to concentrate to get to thirty.

"The agreement was thirty men each," said Hikki quietly. "Freydis has broken it."

Freydis's men were all young and strong, and carried weapons. About half had brought their women. Hekja realized she and Hikki were the only thralls. This was a company of warriors, as well as farmers and hunters. "Perhaps Freydis doesn't trust Finnbogi," she whispered. "Besides, if he doesn't come we will need more than thirty men."

Hikki shrugged. "Maybe she wants to make sure that she is Mistress of Vinland and has the men to back it up. I'm glad," he added. "It is good to be on the winning side."

The oarsmen pushed at their oars. The sail flapped and filled, the cargo boats with their high-piled load of crates and barrels bobbed behind the ship, and suddenly they were away.

"I hated this land," Hekja said. "But I am almost sorry to leave it. It's beautiful in its way."

Hikki shrugged. He was not impressed by beauty. "Land is just something a runner passes through to get to his destination. Leif has promised me land and my freedom, after a year's work with his sister," he added. "Perhaps Freydis will grant you freedom as well."

"Perhaps," said Hekja noncommittally.

"It would be worth working hard to please your

mistress," Hikki added meaningfully. "I can take a wife when I am freed."

Hekja said nothing. She looked around the ship, at Freydis, sitting by the prow, her face glowing as it hadn't done since their last time at sea, at Snorri with his butter hair, sitting at Freydis's side, as though he was storing every second as inspiration to make up a song.

Hekja turned back to Hikki. "But first," she said, "we have to survive."

Chapter 29

The Journey

For Hekja, ships meant storms and icebergs and fog. But this journey was different. Icebergs were plentiful, so Freydis called Snarf to the prow again to sniff them out during the night. But the ship met no fog, or storms. The old man had been right when he told Freydis when to sail.

They sailed straight southwest after that. Leif had sailed further west and come to other lands before he came to Vinland. But now Freydis knew there was land to the south, she had courage enough to shun the coast and cross the open sea. This meant a shorter voyage, even though they had to navigate without a coastline to guide them.

The ship sailed for eight days without a sight of land. Leif had calculated it would take them six, with good winds.

Each day Freydis threw the ship's log into the water and counted slowly as the ship sailed past it.[27]

---

[27] This was the method the Vikings used to tell how fast their ship was going.

The ship was sailing as fast as Leif had expected. But there was still no land.

Nor had there been any rain, and fresh water was running out. Freydis had taken as many barrels as the ship would hold, but the animals needed water too.

People began to mutter. Not loudly, not so Freydis or Thorvard might hear. Norsemen were used to sailing out of sight of land. But they were not used to trusting a woman leader. Thorvard might accompany his wife, but everyone knew whose expedition this really was.

Dusk began to settle on the ninth evening. Freydis handed out the rations: a dried fish each, and a dipper full of water.

"If there had been only thirty men, we would have more than a dipper full to drink," muttered one of the men.

"What did you say?" demanded Freydis sharply.

The man's face was blank. "I said nothing," he said.

"Good," said Freydis. She pulled up another dipperful and handed it to Hekja for Snarf.

Thorvard bent low. "Do you think that is wise?" he whispered, though Hekja could still hear his words. "The other dogs get a quarter ration. The men are talking."

Freydis met his eyes. "If any of the men learn how to sniff an iceberg, they can come and tell me. Till then this dog gets what we do." It was the first time, Hekja thought, that Freydis had openly overruled her husband's advice.

Snarf drank his water, then ate the fish from Hekja's fingers after she'd taken out the bones. Then he dozed, till someone trod on the deck behind them.

Snarf yipped a welcome. It was Snorri the Skald. He shoved a rolled sleeping bag out of the way and sat on the deck next to Hekja. It was the first time he had sought her out since midwinter, though she had sensed him watching her during the voyage.

Was he waiting for her to misbehave, she wondered, so he could tell Freydis of her rudeness to him at Yule? He puzzled her. Most times he acted like any Norseman would. But at others . . .

Snorri looked at Snarf, instead of Hekja, and rubbed his ears, so it almost seemed he had come to talk to the dog rather than to her. "Well, noble hound," he said half jokingly, "can your nose smell out land for us?"

"Arf," said Snarf willingly.

Snorri laughed. "So, you understood that, did you? But was that a yes or a no? What do you say?" he asked Hekja. "Can your dog smell land as well as ice?"

"I don't know," said Hekja honestly. "I think he might be able to."

"It will be useful if he can," said Snorri lightly, but Hekja could hear the urgency behind his words. "Some of the men are saying we've reached the endless ocean, with all hope of land behind us."

"Then you should have stayed safe at home,"

suggested Hekja, then bit her lip. They were harsh words for a thrall to use to a freeman, almost like calling him a coward. Somehow she spoke without thinking when Snorri was around.

But Snorri just raised an eyebrow. Perhaps, he doesn't think I matter enough to be angry at. Then he said, "One day I'll go home again. In a year, perhaps. I'll sing of this voyage and the settling of the land and the adventures. That is what songs do, tell others of what lies beyond their narrow lives."

Hekja said, as though it was no concern of hers, "You don't intend to stay in Vinland, then?"

Snorri looked surprised. "No. I never did. I am my father's heir. One day I must run the estates."

Hekja said nothing. Despite what she had said to Freydis, sometimes, in the dreaming moments before sleep, she had wondered if in this new land a freeman might ask her to be his wife. But if that happened it would not be Snorri the Skald, heir to Norwegian riches.

"What will happen," Hekja said at last, "if we don't find land? Do any of your chants tell of sailors who never found a shore?"

Snorri shook his head. "How could they? My songs have to be about the ones who came safely home, to tell their stories."

"And dead men don't sing songs," said Hekja quietly. "Maybe those alive should sing them for them. Men with dry mouths, aching for rain, their eyes longing for a glimpse of land. Bleached bones floating on old ships, with only the sun and waves to see them."

Snorri was silent for a moment. Then he said, "You almost make it sound like a song."

"No," said Hekja. "These are your heroes, not mine. Nor my songs neither."

"You don't think what we are doing is worth a song?"

Hekja shrugged. "I didn't say that. But your heroes are not my heroes."

"And who would your heroes be?" asked Snorri softly.

Hekja smiled. She laid her hand on Snarf's back and scratched him just above the tail. Snarf stretched in ecstasy and laid his head on her lap.

"Snarf is a hero," said Hekja. "He saved me and my friends from a wolf when he wasn't even full grown. He must have been scared, but he still went for that wolf's throat. Our chief was a hero. He took his boat out in the high seas to save three fishermen. My mother was a hero. Even as they were killing her, she used her last breath to tell me to run. But what do I know of heroes?" added Hekja, "I am just a thrall."

"Arf!" Snarf was barking, his nose in the air. "Arf!"

Hekja rubbed sleep from her eyes. Freydis threw off her sleeping bag, then stood and peered out into the darkness. In a heartbeat Thorvard was at her side.

"He is pointing west," he muttered. "The iceberg

must be far on our right side. There is no need to worry about it." Thorvard slipped into his sleeping bag again.

"Arf!" Snarf barked louder than ever.

"Good dog," said Freydis, absently rubbing his ears. "We've heard you; now go to sleep."

Snarf sat and growled, deep in his throat, then stood and barked again.

Freydis sighed. "Some of us need to sleep. Can't you get him to be quiet, Hekja?"

"No!" urged Hekja. "Please. It's something different. It's not his iceberg bark."

"Arf!" Snarf strained his body toward the west, then looked back as though willing them to understand.

"Please!" Hekja pleaded. "Listen to him!"

Freydis laid her hand on Snarf's head, and gazed into the darkness. Suddenly she seemed to understand. "Land?" asked Freydis softly. "Do you smell land?"

"Woof! Woof! Woof!" Now the other dogs were barking too.

"Hard aport!" yelled Freydis suddenly. "You at the tiller! Move!"

The ship slowly swerved, till it faced the wind. Snarf's nostrils flared, as though whatever he smelled became stronger now. As the ship moved he moved with it, and he kept pointing in the same direction—west.

All over the ship, men woke up and rubbed their eyes. And still he pointed into the darkness. It was only when he was sure that they were headed in the right direction that Snarf sat and rested his nose on Hekja's lap.

Dawn came behind them, the sun rising out of the sea. But even in the faint light before sunrise they had all seen it, like a line of clouds on the horizon.

But these clouds were land.

* * *

Years later Hekja would make a song of how her dog discovered Vinland. Their ship had been headed too far east. If it hadn't been for Snarf's nose they would never have come to land at all.

Of course others had discovered Vinland before Snarf. Hekja would make songs about them too, the Skraelings and Bjarnin Herolfsson then Leif.

But for Hekja, Snarf would always be the true discoverer of Vinland. What did it matter that he was not the first?

Chapter 30

Land!

The land came closer and closer still. The sea changed color, brighter, greener, till Hekja could see waves, all white-tipped about this shore. The wind smelled of soil and trees, more trees than Hekja had thought possible for a land to grow. It was a strangely flat land too, with green hills instead of proper mountains.

By the time the sun was high, they had come in close enough to see the beach. Here was another strangeness—sand that glowed the same color as the sun, not stones or rock. Great beaches stretched to the horizon, instead of coves and fiords where a ship could rest. The ship sailed for a whole day, and all they saw were trees and sand.

But this, it seemed, was what Leif had described. No one minded the lack of water now.

There was no safe harbor where the ship could rest that night—the waves rolled into the shore and the wind was strong. Besides, there seemed to be no streams or rivers where there would be fresh water anyway.

Freydis ordered the sails lowered, though, so the ship didn't drift far in the night. There might be rocks or sandbars, where the ship might run aground, and in any case she was looking for the island that Leif described, that led to Vinland's harbor. It would be easy to miss it sailing on at night.

Dawn saw the ship not much further than they'd been the night before, but the wind was still strong. By mid-morning they discovered Leif's island, sitting like a fat blue whale on the outer edge of a great harbor.

Everyone cheered and clapped each other on the back, as though no one had ever doubted they'd land safely.

Freydis ordered Thorvard to steer to the landward side of the island and told the lookout to watch for sandbanks and rocks. Now they could see a headland, with twisted trees blown out of shape by the wind. Below the headland was a great beach of rippling sand and a river, wider than Hekja had dreamed that any stream could be. Far up the river something gleamed among the trees—the lake that Leif had also described.

Vinland!

Finally it was safe to cross the sandbanks into the mouth of the river.

Hekja peered down into the water. It was so shallow still, she could see the sand, all rippled like the waves had carved it, and a few fish, too, with silver scales that glistened in the shallows. Hekja leaned down and lowered a dipper into the river water and tasted it. "It's salty!" she spluttered, spitting it out.

Freydis grinned. "It's too near the sea. Don't worry; there'll be fresh water further up."

People were shouting now. You could smell the excitement, so strong it could carry the ship to shore without the wind.

"The trees!" cried someone. "Look at the size of the trees!"

"And the ducks! Enough feathers to bed an army!"

"A land of plenty," breathed someone else. It was Hikki. Hekja could almost hear his dreams: land here, and far richer than any he had known.

"It's beautiful," said a voice behind her. It was Snorri.

Hekja nodded. "The colors—it is all gold and green and blue. Like every color has been dyed twice to make it glow."

Suddenly the men gave a cheer. There on the river banks, in a clearing among the tall, tall trees, were the two big longhouses that Leif had built and promised to his sister. There were smaller huts for smelleding iron and carpentry and storerooms.

As they drew closer, she noticed smoke sifting into the sky above the green sod roofs. There was another boat pulled up in the shallows.

We're here, thought Hekja. And Finnbogi has arrived before us.

Chapter 31

The First Night in Vinland

Finnbogi's men came running out of the longhouses and in from the forest, to stare at the ship as it came up the river. Thorvard pulled it close enough to the bank to cast a rope ashore, and one of Finnbogi's men tied it around a tree. Another shoved out a plank so the passengers could come ashore.

Freydis's men and women clambered onto the dry land. There was more back-slapping; men gulped river water and splashed their faces to wash off the salt. They paced around the trees, exclaiming at their size. The women marveled at the lush grass and what milk and cheese the cows would give on such a pasture.

But Freydis stood back as the others rushed to shore. Even now she stared down the coast, past the great river, as though wondering what new lands might be there. She caught Hekja watching her and smiled slightly.

Hekja stood back to let her pass, holding Snarf by

the scruff of the neck to stop him bounding out, and let the others climb out first. She watched as Freydis stepped across the gangplank and narrowed her eyes at the smoke coming from the longhouse's smoke hole.

"Men," she muttered. "That's all that Finnbogi has brought, it seems. Where are the women, hey? Thorvard!"

Thorvard had been staring around the clearing. "What is it?"

"Tell the men to fetch their weapons," said Freydis in a low voice. "One by one, so no one notices."

Thorvard stared. "What's wrong?"

"Where are Finnbogi's cattle? His sheep?"

"Perhaps he thought he would share ours," said Thorvard.

"Exactly," said Freydis quietly. "Whether we agreed or not."

Thorvard's eyes widened. "I will tell the men," he said softly.

Hekja shivered. Was their new life to begin with killing?

Freydis beckoned to her. "Come with me," she ordered. She started for the longhouse.

They reached the longhouse just as Finnbogi stepped out.

"Welcome," he said, grinning. "We made it here before you!" He waved a hand at the giant trees, the grass that looked like it had never known the snow of winter. "It is just as Leif described! Even the grapes, great bunches of them on thick vines, hanging from the trees."

Freydis ignored the talk of grapes. "Why didn't you call at Brattahlid, as we agreed?"

Finnbogi's grin grew wider. "Is that what we agreed? I must have forgotten."

"It was," said Freydis coldly. She looked around. "I see your men, Finnbogi, but no women. No cattle, either. How can you settle a new land with neither cows nor women?"

Finnbogi looked down on her from his great height. He looked like he was enjoying himself. "A man can make riches with neither cows nor women. Besides, my wife is here, and her thralls. That is enough for me."

"And for your men?"

Finnbogi shrugged, and glanced at Hekja. "If you have brought women, then perhaps we'll have to share."

Hekja felt her skin prickle. But she gave no sign that she had understood.

"We will share profits," said Freydis crisply, "and that is all. Why have you put your belongings here?"

"Where else?" Finnbogi looked her up and down lazily.

"These houses are my brother's," said Freydis. "He said that I could use them—me and my people."

Finnbogi shrugged, his grin even wider. "Then you should have set out earlier. You can build your own houses. I am here now, me and my men."

"I have men of my own," said Freydis evenly.

"Men who follow a woman," snorted Finnbogi.

"My men followed me to Vinland. They will follow me now," said Freydis quietly.

"Then perhaps you should have brought them with you," said Finnbogi.

"We are partners, Finnbogi," said Freydis, still in that too quiet voice. "Do I need men with me for you to honor your word?"

The two stood there. If they had been dogs, they would have growled, thought Hekja, their hackles raised. But these two only stared.

"Do not cross me, Finnbogi," said Freydis finally. "My men have their swords and axes and are waiting for my word. Where are your men's weapons? Hanging up inside the houses? You have a choice. We can start this colony with your men's blood upon the ground. Or you can leave my longhouses, according to the law."

Finnbogi stared at her for a moment without speaking. Then he pushed past her, out onto the path down to the river. Hekja heard him shouting at his men to leave the unloading and come and take their things from the longhouse.

Freydis smiled, but her eyes were worried.

* * *

Finnbogi's clan loaded their belongings back onto their ship.

"Watch them," Freydis told Hekja. "I want to know exactly where they go."

Hekja ran out to the bend of the river and watched Finnbogi sail further down the shore, then into the lake. The trees were too tall to see where they headed after that, but soon smoke rose up into the air. It seemed Finnbogi had set up camp on the lakeshore. Hekja ran back to tell Freydis.

The cattle had been unloaded now, though their legs were unsteady after the voyage. Freydis ordered the bull tethered to a tree, while young branches were stripped from the trees Finnbogi's men had cut to make a rough fence to keep the cattle and sheep in. The hen boxes were placed on a platform of big rocks, and the hens let loose to scratch around. They would roost in the trees at night and come back to their boxes to lay.

"Come," said Freydis to Hekja again. They left the others to their unloading and entered the biggest of the longhouses.

It was far larger than the farmhouse in Greenland, and twice as high, with a framework of great tree trunks, and wooden walls as well. There was a big attic room where the men could sleep. There were storerooms and the hall below, and bed closets closed off by wooden walls, for the couples. Hekja had never seen those before. There was a big room at the end of the great hall for Freydis and Thorvard. All along the hall were benches of rough wood to sit on and half-round slabs of wood resting on tree trunks for tables.

The fire pit was massive too—there was certainly no shortage of wood to burn in this rich land. Finnbogi's fire was still burning in the fire pit.

"Tell the women to build the fire up high," ordered Freydis. "Then they can choose their bed closet."

Hekja nodded. She supposed that if the couples slept in the closets, she would sleep alone in the great hall, with Snarf. Hekja went out to give the orders. They were the first she had ever given, but no one seemed to notice.

Some of the men had already caught salmon in their nets in the river—giant fish that glistened in the sun. You only had to throw in a net, they said, for it to fill up with fish. Soon the salmon were hanging on the roasting chains above the fire, tended by the women. Freydis ordered a barrel of barley beer be broached, to celebrate their arrival. One by one the men came in and sat before the fire, with horns of ale and platters of cooked fish. And then Thorvard carried in the great carved chair that had sat by the fire pit in the farmhouse in Greenland. He placed it in the spot of honor, facing south. The men waited for him to sit in it. But instead he sat on one of the benches, like the other men.

Then Freydis entered. She walked steadily up the hall, to the fire pit, then sat in the great chair, just as though she were a man.

No one spoke. The silence grew, then Snorri's voice rose clearly through the dimness of the longhouse. He had left the harp in Greenland, as he had promised. But Snorri had no need of a harp, thought Hekja.

"Over the trackless ocean,
 Over the endless sea,
 Food for ravens we traveled,
 But none flew as far as we.

"Warriors boast of beating,
 Weaker foes than ours.
 A man's strength is fleeting,
 Against an ocean's powers.

"Now we have a new land,
 Ours to change and watch and grow.
 Let only they who dare to follow,
 Question how we go."

No one cheered. The words meant too much for them to toast the singer, so they gave him the even greater compliment of silence. Hekja stared across the fire at Snorri, heir to great estates, further from her than Bran had ever been.

And so she spent her first night in Vinland, in a house much like the one that she had left. The men snored in their sleeping bags above, the couples whispered in the bed closets. The smoke drifted lazily until it found the smoke hole, and outside, the roosters crowed, taking the moonlight for the sun.

Chapter 32

Exploring Vinland

The next morning Freydis wasted no time giving her orders. Some men were to put up more fencing, for the cows would calve soon and the ewes would have their lambs, and all the animals would need more grass. Other men were sent to hunt, for the party needed fresh meat as well as fish. The last of the men would build byres for the animals, to shelter them when winter came. The women were to feed and tend the animals, set up the looms, and choose where the summer crops could be sown, so the grain had time to ripen before winter.

Leif had said that animals could be left out in this mild land, as there would be grass for them to eat all winter long. But Freydis wanted to take no chances. It was a long way to Greenland to get more cows or sheep.

The animals were eating as though they had never seen grass like this before. Hekja grinned. She supposed they hadn't. Even the bull didn't lift his head when she walked past to fill a bucket from the river. She was carrying it back when Hikki came jogging over to find her. He looked happier than she had ever seen him.

"Come on!" he yelled. "It is time for us to run the land!"

Hekja went back inside and changed into the running dress that Freydis had given her. It had two loops and buttons to fasten the material between her legs and at the sides, but her arms were bare. The women stared at her and giggled as they shook out the sleeping bags, but Hekja paid no attention. She was stronger and faster than those house women would ever be.

Freydis looked her up and down, then nodded.

"Tell Hikki to come in," she ordered.

Hikki had changed into his running shift, too. He looked even more different from the big, fair Norsemen now. His strong runner's legs were so unlike the muscles of the men who exercised with sword and axe. He nodded respectfully to Freydis. "Which way should we run, mistress?"

"Run south along the coast for two days," ordered Freydis. "Then inland for two days, then run four days north, and make your way back along the coast. But if there is anything worth investigating, you may take longer."

"What sort of thing, mistress?" asked Hikki.

"Birds' nests, lakes of fish. My brother said that

there were fields of wild grain and berries. There's a whole land out there waiting to be discovered," Freydis said softly. "And you will see it first and tell me all about it."

"We are to run both together?" asked Hikki.

Freydis nodded. "If one has an accident, the other can help." She smiled at Hekja. "And yes, you can take the dog, too. But be warned," she said quietly to Hikki, so none of the house women could hear her words, "if you so much as look at her, I will pull your guts out through your mouth and feed them to the fishes."

Hikki glanced at Hekja, then back at Freydis. "I would never do anything without your permission, mistress."

"See you don't," said Freydis, amused.

Hikki set off at a jog as soon as they were outside. Hekja followed him, with Snarf bounding happily at her side. The whole camp stopped work, it seemed, to watch them go. Hekja could feel their eyes on her bare legs.

Snorri was stripping bark from a fallen tree for the new fencing, just beyond the clearing. He must have just chopped it down, for his axe lay next to his shirt. Hekja nodded at him politely as she passed, and Snarf gave him a happy "arf'. Snorri only nodded in reply. It wasn't till she passed that she heard him call, "Take care!"

She stopped, and turned. He was still staring at

her. "Would you tell a warrior going to battle to take care?" she asked.

Snorri frowned. "No." And then he grinned. "Though maybe I should. Come back safe," he added, and now he didn't grin.

Hekja felt herself blushing. "I will." She turned back, and followed Hikki through the trees.

* * *

It was easy running on that first morning. This time Hekja carried a pack like Hikki's, with a cloak, knife, a water bladder, and another bladder filled with oatmeal mixed with salt butter. Hikki also carried flint and ironstone.

The sun was barely high when they reached the beach. They ran along the sand where it was firmest, just above the waves. For a while there was little to see, for the sand dunes rose between them and the land. All that was visible were the scattered islands, most no larger than a whale. They passed piles of rotting seaweed for Snarf to nose at. The sand was almost the color of the sun. The waves rolled smoothly and splashed their ankles.

When the sun was high, Hikki announced a rest stop. They crossed the sand dunes, up into the edges of the forest, where the sand met the first black soil. There they flopped down into the shade. Snarf shook himself—wet sand flying from his fur into their faces—then he flopped too. He had found a dead seagull and had carried it proudly in his mouth for the last part of their run.

Hekja kicked it further away. "If you're going to eat that," she said firmly, "you can sit over there."

"Arf," said Snarf reproachfully. He trotted over to his seagull and sat down to chew it.

Hekja opened her pack and pulled out her water bladder[28] for a few gulps. She rested against a tree and shut her eyes and when she opened them Hikki was staring at her.

"You don't use your arms," he said abruptly.

"My what?"

"Your arms. When you run. That is why you are so tired now. You need to let your body balance, so it pulls you along."

"I don't understand," said Hekja.

Hikki shrugged. Then he said, "The singer . . . what do you think of him?"

Hekja hesitated. "I think he has the most wonderful voice I have ever heard," she said honestly, and watched Hikki's face darken. "I also think he is a Norseman, and my enemy."

"Perhaps. But you still have to live with these people," said Hikki. He studied her face closely.

"I know," said Hekja softly. "For a while I hoped I could go back home. But my home no longer exists. If I ever have a home again, it will be here. But not with a Norseman."

Hikki smiled at her. "Come on," he said. "Now I

---

[28] a calf's bladder that was scraped clean and kept soaked in water so it didn't dry out till it was needed

will show you how to be the finest runner in the world."

* * *

Before she'd met Hikki, Hekja had thought that all you needed to run well was strong legs and some practice running after cows. Now she learned differently.

This time, as they ran along the beach, Hikki showed her how to push with her bare toes, swing her arms, and angle her body against the wind so it almost seemed that she might fall, but somehow she ran faster, and easier, too.

Most of all he showed her how to pace herself, so that she ran at an easy speed without having to stop and rest. Suddenly it seemed as though their feet ate up the beach, as headland after headland disappeared behind them.

That night, when they set up a place to camp, Hekja stared at the creatures Hikki had placed over the coals of the fire.

"What are they?"

"Crabs. One of Leif's men told me about them. They have their bones outside, not inside. They're supposed to taste like fish."

They did. Hekja poked the last of the flesh from the claws while the furry creature cooked, and Snarf gulped the guts, then settled down to doze, with one ear up so he didn't miss anything and his nose pointing away from the fire so he could smell the new scents.

"It's beautiful," said Hekja at last. "The golden sand and the waves. I never thought anywhere could be so beautiful. Do you think we are the first people ever to see this?"

Hikki shrugged. "Maybe. Leif's party explored too. But it is a rich land, true enough. There is wealth enough for everybody here." Then he added, "My muscles are sore—they grew too soft aboard the ship." He stood and began to undo his tunic.

Hekja stared. "What are you doing?"

Hikki grinned at her. "I'm going to bathe. Have you ever tried it?"

Hekja shook her head.

"It stops your muscles from aching," said Hikki. He shrugged and added carefully, "But the waves are probably too rough for a girl."

Hekja glared at him. "If you can bathe, I can too."

She undid a button on her tunic, and then looked up. Hikki was still staring at her. "Look away!" she ordered.

Hikki grinned. "Why?"

"Because Freydis ordered it," said Hekja. Then she added, "And because I ask you to."

"Then I will obey you, not Freydis, this time," said Hikki seriously.

Hikki pretended to look at the sky while Hekja undressed, then raced down the sand without looking behind. Hekja followed him. They waded out till the waves crashed against their waists. Hikki ducked down till only his head was showing. Hekja copied him, while Snarf splashed at the shallows, looking worried.

"It's cold! But good!" yelled Hekja.

"I told you it was," said Hikki smugly.

Hekja wondered if he could see her shape under the water. But she could only dimly make out the white of his body, so she supposed the water hid her, too. The last naked man Hekja had seen had been her older brother, years before, but that was different.

They ran back after that, Hekja first, then Hikki when she called that she was dressed. They sat by the fire while the shadows grew deeper. They talked of the villages where they had been taken from, and of the families that now were dead. It was the first time that Hekja had talked so freely since her capture, and somehow it seemed to take away some of the pain.

Hikki talked too about the farm he'd have soon, when Freydis gave him land and freedom. But Hekja never mentioned that Freydis had said she would free her, too.

The moon hovered above them, so bright it made shadows, just like the sun. Hikki leaned over and threw more wood on the fire. An owl hooted. It sounded strangely like an owl from home.

Down on the beach the waves pounded out their own music. And suddenly Hekja felt a new song sweep through her. The words had come to her as she had run that afternoon, but now the tune carried them along.

"My heart was crying,
  As they took me from my home,
  But my mouth made no sound.
  I would not sing for Norsemen,
  Not of sorrow or of joy.

"Today our heels have flown,
  Across white sand and gold,
  Today my soul is free,
  And I can sing again."

The music died away. Hikki gazed at her, his mouth open as though it was the first song he had ever heard. Finally he said softly, "The Norsemen prize good singing. You would not have had to mind the cows if they knew that you could sing like that."

"My singing is mine, not theirs," said Hekja, just as she had said to Snorri with his butter hair.

"But still . . ." began Hikki.

"No," said Hekja. The song had left her empty. "No discussion."

They headed northwards now, as Freydis had instructed, over low hills, along animal trails again that were hidden among the trees. Suddenly Snarf stopped, and barked. "Arf!" It was his danger call.

Hekja looked back. "What is it, boy?" she demanded.

"Arf!" Snarf barked again, then growled warningly.

Hekja looked around. But there was nothing to see.

Snarf growled again.

"What's wrong with him?" called Hikki.

Hekja shook her head. "I don't know," she admitted. "I can't see anything. It must be something he can smell." She bent and patted Snarf's head.

"Maybe he's hungry," suggested Hikki.

"Maybe," said Hekja doubtfully. She gazed around again, but there seemed to be nothing wrong, so they began to run again.

Snarf bounded after her. But he seemed wary now, no longer leaping carelessly through the trees or bringing back branches for Hekja to toss.

That night they slept on a hill above a marshy lake, but Snarf only dozed.

Chapter 33

The Skraelings

When Hekja woke at dawn, Snarf was awake, his hackles raised, and growling. "What is it, boy?" whispered Hekja, sitting up in her sleeping bag. Hikki was still asleep.

Snarf whined, and pointed into the forest with his nose.

"Hikki, I think you should . . ." began Hekja in her normal voice.

Snarf whined again more urgently, to tell her to be quiet. This time she understood.

"What's wrong?" she whispered. And then she smelled it too.

Smoke.

Their fire had been out for hours, so the smoke could not be theirs. She pushed her way out of her sleeping bag in alarm and looked around.

Snarf pointed again, the way Thorvard had shown him. Hekja nodded, and crawled over to Hikki. "Wake up!" she whispered. "Shh! Wake up!"

Hikki knows how to be silent, thought Hekja—years as a thrall will teach you that. He woke up blinking but didn't speak till Hekja whispered, "Smoke!"

"Where?" hissed Hikki.

Snarf growled, deep and low, and walked forward a few steps and looked around, as though to say, "Follow me."

Hikki beckoned to Hekja. "Place your feet down on their outsides like this," he whispered as he demonstrated what he meant. "It's quieter that way. Move your body as little as you can, especially your head—it's movement that attracts attention."

Hekja nodded. They grabbed their packs and followed Snarf through the trees and then around a hill.

And then they saw them. It was a hunting party of seven men, and dogs, too. Now Hekja knew why Snarf had led them upwind—so the dogs wouldn't smell them as he had smelled the fire and cooking meat.

The men's fire was nearly out, but they had been feasting well. A deer's carcass, mostly charred bones, lay next to its pelt. It was rolled up to carry away, and there was another carcass hanging from a tree.

The hunters looked different from any men that Hekja had ever seen. Their hair was long and black instead of red or blond like the Greenlanders, or brown like Hekja's and Hikki's. They were shorter than Norsemen too, and had darker skin. They were dressed in softly fringed skins, tied above their chests or around their waists, and their hair was shaved to make a long crest on top. Feathers poked behind their ears, and they wore strange markings on their wrists, legs, and chests.

Hekja froze, hardly breathing. She knew how Snarf felt now, for the hair on the back of her neck rose at the scent of danger, just like his.

The men called lazily to each other as they picked up their supplies. They moved off, down the hill. Hekja stayed perfectly still until she heard their calls slowly die away.

"Who were they?" she breathed.

"Skraelings," muttered Hikki. The word just meant "natives' or ones who lived in this place. "Leif's men didn't mention Skraelings."

"We have to follow them," whispered Hekja. "We need to know more."

Hikki hesitated. "If we get too close they'll hear us, or the dogs will smell us if the wind changes suddenly. These men are hunters." He looked at Snarf, staring through the trees, and came to a decision. "We'd best wait, till they get a distance away, and trust Snarf to track them. Can he do that?"

Hekja nodded.

"Follow, boy!" she whispered. Snarf put his nose to the ground on command.

It was easier than Hekja had thought it would be. Snarf moved quietly and confidently through the forest, until the Skraeling village was below them.

"It's enormous!" whispered Hikki.

Hekja nodded. This village was even bigger than Brattahlid. The houses were quite different from any she had seen—made of tree branches with rounded roofs.

All around the houses there were fields, with tall yellow flowers[29], green-leaved plants[30] and grain[31] higher than a Norseman's head. Smoke from cooking fires rose into the air.

And people. More people than she had ever seen!

The men were dressed like the hunters, but there were women, too, with bare feet and breasts, leather skirts and strings of beads. Their heads were also shaved across the top, and there were markings on their skin just like the men's. The children were mostly naked, running around the village, yelling and playing games.

Hikki and Hekja looked at each other, then edged back into the trees. Then they ran as swiftly as they could, back the way they came.

* * *

The sun was low on the horizon before they stopped. "Freydis has to know of this at once," said Hekja.

Hikki nodded. This land had a people—and they looked like warriors, too.

"It's a good land, Hekja. Worth fighting for."

Hekja looked up at that. "Fighting!" she whispered.

---

[29] sunflowers
[30] several types of pumpkins and gourds, tobacco, beans and spinach
[31] maize

Hikki looked surprised. "Of course. That is what the Norsemen do. They fought for land in Ireland and England and the islands. They drove off the first Icelanders to take the land instead. So they will fight the Skraelings for this land, too." He shrugged. "Did you notice? The Skraelings had no iron weapons. The Norsemen do."

"But there is plenty of land here! Enough for everyone!"

"Norsemen fight," said Hikki, as though this explained it all.

"But Freydis is in charge now," said Hekja slowly. "Maybe . . . maybe things will be different."

Hikki shrugged.

Hekja looked out, through the trees to the hills beyond, with the glint of water and the glades of grass. "It is so beautiful," she said softly. "It seems impossible there should be hatred and violence here. Does every land have its own beauty? The crags of the mountain at home, the islands of rain and sun in the gray sea, the white of the ice against the sky in Greenland, the green and richness here. All different, all beautiful."

Finally Hekja stood up. "Come on. We've rested enough." She grinned at him wickedly. "Or are you too tired to keep running?"

Hikki glared at her for a moment, his pride stung, then realized she was joking. "I'll race you to the next hill," he offered.

Hekja grinned and shook her head. "No competition. You run faster than I do Hikki, I admit it."

"I'll give you a head start. Come on, go!"

Hekja ran. Snarf bounded with her. She could hear Hikki running too, but could tell that he wasn't running his fastest.

Hekja made the hill first. She turned to wait for Hikki, laughing. "You are getting old, Hikki!" she taunted.

Hikki smiled. "No," he said simply, "my life is just beginning."

By mid-afternoon Freydis's camp was below them. Hekja began to trot down the hill, but Hikki put his hand on her arm. It was the first time he had touched her since they had left the camp. "Stay a moment," he said.

Hekja turned. "Why?"

For the first time Hikki looked embarrassed. "Would you sing again?" he whispered. "A song from our land, a song like my mother might have sung."

Hekja smiled. She sat on a log and looked out over the camp and the river to the sea, just as she might have looked out at the harbor from her ma's doorway. This time she sang a song that her ma had taught her, about a fisherman who caught a seal with a gold ring in its mouth.

The fisherman knew this was no ordinary seal. He kept the ring and let the seal go, and as it swam through the water it turned into a beautiful woman.

The woman swam back to his boat and held up her arms to him. The fisherman married her, and from that day no fisherman of their family was ever drowned.

Hikki watched as Hekja sang, then Snarf joined in. "Arooooh!"

Hekja began to giggle, and even Hikki laughed. Suddenly Snarf leaped to his feet. "Arf Arf!"

For a moment Hekja thought it might be Skraelings again. Then she realized this was a bark of welcome.

It was Snorri. He had been cutting timber, for he carried his axe and he smelled of wood sap as well as sweat. He had been standing behind them as she sang.

"I thought you wouldn't sing for anyone?"

"Not for a Norseman," said Hekja softly. Then, without asking Snorri's leave, she began to run down the hill.

"Master," began Hikki, unsure of what to say.

"Go," said Snorri shortly.

Hekja could feel his eyes on them as they ran down the hill to Freydis.

Freydis was checking the new sheep fields. The sheep had been shorn recently, and were due to lamb, and the new fences had to be closely woven to stop the lambs from wriggling through them.

She leaned against the fence and stared at them. "Well?" she demanded. "What's wrong?" She smiled slightly as Hikki gaped. "You are back before I told you to return. It's not much of a guess that you found out something I need to know at once."

Hekja let Hikki talk—he had more experience than she did in fitting all that had happened into a short account. Freydis looked thoughtful when he had finished.

"Fetch Thorvard," she said at last to Hikki.

"Should I go?" offered Hekja.

"No," said Freydis. "Stay." She questioned Hekja again about every detail of the Skraeling camp till Thorvard arrived, and then they had to tell their story again.

Thorvard listened in silence too. And then he grinned. "So," he said, "we fight."

"No," said Freydis flatly.

Thorvard stared at her. "If we want this land, we have to take it!"

Freydis shook her head. "This isn't like Ireland, or England or the islands, with the best land taken. There is rich land enough here for us and the Skraelings, too. Besides, we have no reinforcements here. We have only forty men. . . ."

"And Finnbogi's," put in Thorvard softly.

"And Finnbogi's. But from what the runners say, the Skraelings have more men than in the whole of Brattahlid ten times over. There is no way we can take this land by force."

"We are not cowards—" Thorvard began.

"It has nothing to do with cowardice!" interrupted Freydis. "If I thought we could defeat them, I'd say let's attack their village now, take them by surprise, and burn it to the ground. But where there is one village, there will be more."

"Then what do we do?" asked Thorvard unwillingly.

"We wait here until they find us," said Freydis flatly. "And we try to look like friends, not enemies."

Chapter 34

The Skraelings Arrive

It took the Skraelings half a moon to find the Norse camp.

It was early morning when they paddled their skin-covered canoes up the estuary to the river. They came slowly, as though they were in no hurry. Hekja had plenty of time to find Freydis after the lookout called.

As the canoes drew closer, some of the Skraelings put their oars down and waved sticks that made a noise like the sound of barley flails that blew the chaff off the grain.

Freydis shaded her eyes and stared at them.

"What do you think?" she whispered to Thorvard.

Thorvard stared out at the massed canoes. "I think each man needs to fetch his weapons," he muttered. "There are more than twice our number there."

Beside him Snorri gazed, fascinated by the newcomers. "Maybe the noise is a sign of peace," he said. "If they were going to attack, surely they'd try to be quiet."

Freydis flashed him a smile. "My thinking, too, skalder boy. Go fetch the white shield hanging by the fire," she ordered Snorri. "Maybe they will recognize it as a sign of peace. And yes," she added to Thorvard, "tell the men to fetch their weapons too, but two at a time only, so the Skraelings don't think we are preparing for a battle. The women are to stay in the longhouse."

Hekja wondered whether that meant she was to go to the longhouse too. But Freydis made no sign that she was to leave, so she stayed where she was. Snorri came running with the shield. Freydis held it high, while all the camp gathered behind her. Each man had his shield and sword or battle-axe ready to hand, but on Freydis's orders held them low, so as to not look too ready for war.

Hikki edged up to Hekja. "If they attack, run toward the hills," he whispered. "We can hide among the trees."

Hekja stared at him. He shrugged. "The free men have their swords and axes. We have nothing but our legs."

When the Skraelings leaped out and pulled their canoes up onto the bank, their leader strode toward Freydis. He was taller than the other Skraelings, almost Viking size, with many strings of big white beads[32] about his neck. He stared at the cows as though he had never seen cattle before, then he

---

[32] pearls

stepped up to Thorvard and said something.

The words made no sense to Hekja. Thorvard shook his head too. The Skraeling leader nodded, as though he had expected this. He signaled to his men.

The Skraelings pulled out piles of pelts from the boats and carried them over to their chief, then put them down at Thorvard's feet.

Thorvard glanced at Freydis. She handed the white shield back to Snorri and picked up one of the pelts and stroked it. She nodded at Thorvard. "These are good furs. It seems he wants to trade."

The chief pointed to Thorvard's sword and said something sharply.

Freydis stepped forward. "No," she said, and though the chief must have found the word strange, her meaning was obvious. "We will not trade fur for weapons."

The chief spoke again, more angrily. He pointed again at Thorvard's sword, as Skraelings yelled behind him, stamping their feet on the ground. Hikki began to edge away. "Time to run," he said to Hekja.

"Not yet," said Hekja urgently. "Stop! If we run now, the Skraelings will think that we are scared."

Freydis beckoned Hekja.

"Fetch some cheeses," she ordered. "Quickly! And fresh milk as well."

Hekja ran. She yelled to one of the women staring from the longhouse doorway to bring out a bucket of milk, while she grabbed a cheese, a big one nearly ripe, and carried it to Freydis, Thorvard, and the chief. Behind her two of the women struggled with great buckets of fresh milk.

Slowly, very slowly, so there should be no misunderstanding, Freydis pulled out the small knife from the chain that dangled from her brooch. She cut a wedge of cheese, sliced off a tiny piece, and put it in her mouth. Then she handed the rest of the wedge to the chief.

The chief sniffed it suspiciously, then bit it.

He smiled.

Freydis smiled too. She took a bucket of milk from the women behind her and handed that to the big man too, with a gesture for him to drink.

The chief lifted the bucket. Hekja heard him gulping. When he finally put it down, his smile was even wider.

It was easy after that. The Skraelings brought out more bales of pelts from their canoes and Freydis emptied the dairy of milk, cheese and butter to trade for them.

"There will be no cheese for us," whispered Hikki, staring as fascinated as the rest.

"No matter," said Hekja. "Vinland has more than enough food." She gazed at Freydis. "She was wonderful. The Skraeling didn't even look at her. But she made him see that she was in command. They could have killed us all. But instead they are leaving us with furs—and all for cheese."

"Indeed," said a voice. It was Snorri the Skald. Somehow he always seemed to be near Hekja now, though whenever she glanced at him he was looking somewhere else.

Hekja turned, as though she hadn't known that he was there. "Worthy of a song?" she asked softly.

Snorri stared at her for a moment without speaking. Then he said, "Perhaps. Or perhaps a woman should sing about another woman's deeds."

Chapter 35

Vinland Days

The Skraelings came often after that. They brought more furs and, as the summer melted into autumn, some of their strange grains as well. One grew on long stalks and could be cooked when young and tender, or ground to flour when it was older.[33] Another kind came from flowers[34] and were eaten raw, or made into an oily paste like butter.

They brought gourds, too—dried ones carved with strange designs for storage, and others that were sweet, soft, and yellow inside when they were cooked.[35]

If there wasn't enough milk or cheese, they traded for strips of bright red cloth, which they tied around their heads. But milk and cheese were prized more than anything else the Norse folk had.

Snorri the Skald began to conduct the trading. Unlike the other Norsemen, he was learning

---

[33] maize
[34] sunflower kernels
[35] pumpkin

Skraeling words. The Skraelings even took him hunting. They showed him how to shoot at giant salmon with their stone-tipped arrows. In return, Snorri showed them how the Greenlanders dug fish traps in the sand, which filled with fish at each low tide as the waves retreated down the beach.

"Do the Skraelings have music, too?" Hekja asked Snorri one day. She had seen him climbing across the sandhills, trying to balance two big baskets of the clams the Skraelings had shown him how to dig. It was only polite, she told herself, to run and help him carry them.

Snorri grinned as he passed over the smaller basket. "Not like ours. The first time I heard one of their songs, I thought the man had stuck an arrow in his foot! But they thought the same of my songs."

"They didn't like them?"

Snorri's grin grew even wider at her surprise. "No! Too different. But when I heard their music again—I don't know; I still can't say I enjoy it. But I can see it has a beauty, a complexity, of its own. It is like the Skraelings themselves, Hekja!"

"How?" asked Hekja.

Snorri turned to her eagerly. "They are different too. As different from us as this land is from Norway, or Iceland, or Greenland. The more I see of them, the more fascinating I find them!" He laughed, and threw his hair back over his shoulders. "To think I came here thinking I could only make songs about a new land! Now I can sing about a new people, too, when I go home to Norway."

So he was still planning to leave. They were nearly at the longhouses now. Snarf bounded out to meet them. He had been supervising the young lambs, making sure they knew that dogs were boss.

"Hekja," began Snorri. "If you would like . . . I mean, I could tell you more about the Skraelings, perhaps. . . ."

"I'm sorry," said Hekja hurriedly. "I must see if Freydis has any orders for me. I'll put these by the fire pit tonight." She forced a smile. "I think there is roast deer, as well as a salmon, and Helga has made a bread with the first of the new wheat, and a flummery.[36] There is so much to eat in Vinland, it's hard to know what to taste first!" She walked off too fast for him to reply.

This was indeed a land of plenty. Hekja heard the women commenting that the new fields had given more barley and wheat than any in Greenland or Iceland or Norway. The cows and calves were so fat, they almost rolled around on the grass.

The crops of oats and wheat had been brought in, more than twice as much as similar fields would have given back in Greenland. As the weather cooled, great flocks of swans, geese, ducks, and cranes flew to the estuary, so many that the men boasted they could throw a spear with their eyes shut and still hit two or

---

[36] oat or wheat flour set like a sweet jelly

more. The longhouses smelled richly of roasting meats and bread.

The storerooms were full of skins to trade back in Greenland when the ice about its shores cleared enough next summer. There were great lengths of timber, too, felled and dressed and left to cure on rocky platforms.

The people in the longhouses slept on bearskins now, or even softer furs, and ate from platters of carved gourd. Even Snarf had a carved gourd to lap his water from. Hekja had seen Snorri carve it. But he had never given it to her, just filled it with water and left it where Snarf would find it.

Hekja made sure she avoided him now. Even if friendship between a thrall and a skald was possible, it would only lead to loss next spring.

But life was still good—better, in many ways, than it had ever been. She had responsibility now, and friends, and Snarf. Snarf had filled out even more in the Vinland summer. His chest was broader than a wolf's now and his legs much longer. None of the Greenland dogs was anywhere near his size.

Several of the women were pregnant, too. Soon we will be a proper village, thought Hekja longingly, with children running between the houses. There were plans for more buildings. This colony would grow, just as Greenland had, but faster and more prosperously, for Greenland was a poor land compared to this.

It was almost coming to seem like home.

Chapter 36

Winter Feasting

The first leaves were changing color when Freydis ordered a feast.

"The best of everything," she said to Hekja. "Three days from now. Tell the men we need meat to roast, deer and bear and swans. We will have wheat bread and barley beer, and the first of the young wine. Vinland wine from Vinland grapes!"

Hekja nodded. Then she said, "Why?"

Freydis frowned. "Why what?"

"Why have a feast now?"

Freydis smiled at her. "Always questions. Anyone could guess you were never born to be a thrall! Because I say so." Her smiled deepened. "There is another reason too. But I will announce that at the feast."

"I will give the orders," promised Hekja. She hesitated, then asked, "Should we ask Finnbogi's people, too?"

Freydis frowned. "I have given a lot of thought to

that. No, I don't think so. It would be different if the Skraelings were unfriendly, if we needed to join with Finnbogi to fight them off. But Finnbogi will never accept my authority. It's best to keep our groups apart."

The fires were lit at first light, and by the time the sun had risen high, the coals were ready for the meat. All through the morning the women loaded the big tables with wheat and oat breads, the roasted Skraeling corn and pumpkins, the shellfish, and wheat puddings sweetened with grape juice and rich with eggs. The grease from the roast meat caused the flames to flicker higher and lick against the meat. The smell of cooking filled the camp.

By afternoon everything was ready. Hekja helped the other women serve, and kept the drinking horns filled too. The dogs lay underneath the tables and, as the men got drunker, they fed on the spilled puddings and bones. This time Freydis didn't serve with the other women, but sat in the great carved chair and was waited on, like a chief.

When the best of the meat had been eaten, Snorri the Skald stood up. Hekja had noticed he had drunk less than the other men, and eaten less too. The men quietened, even those who had been arguing at the tops of their voices. The sun began to sink in a golden haze. Snorri began to sing.

He sang to Freydis, at the head of the tables. It was a song about a prince who had to defeat the enemies who had stolen his kingdom and his family and the princess he was to marry. He met a white swan, who showed him where the forest kept its treasure, so he could have enough silver to pay an army. The swan flew above the enemy camp, so the prince knew where his army should wait in ambush. When the prince finally won the battle the swan taught him a song to sing to his princess, to tell her he loved her.

Then the swan flew away, and the hero realized it was the swan that he had loved all the time.

And so Snorri sang, his butter-colored hair gleaming in the moonlight:

> *" Across the sea I came wandering,*
> *For glory and heroes and fame,*
> *But I knew not for what I was searching,*
> *For love was only a name."*

Finally the swan heard the prince calling her from across the mountains. She flew back and the lovers were reunited. They were swans in summer, flying across the world. In winter they turned into a prince and princess and lived in the prince's kingdom.

Hekja's eyes were bright when the song had finished. He didn't even look at her, but somehow she knew that the song was meant for her. She stared at Snorri across the fire, hoping no one could see her in the dark.

Freydis stood and waved her horn mug in the air to

silence the cheering. "Thank you, Snorri the Skald," she cried, "for brightening our feast. Maybe one day you will judge our deeds to be worthy of a song too!"

The men cheered again. Someone called for another song, but Freydis waved him silent.

"There will be time enough for singing," she called. "But now I have an announcement."

The whole crowd was quiet now. Did Freydis plan another expedition, to explore further still? Hekja remembered Freydis staring at the sea to the south, on their first day in Vinland.

But Freydis smiled, and said, "This land has given us riches beyond our dreams. Soon it will give me something more. For in five months, Thorvard and I will have a child."

The cheering nearly lifted the roofs off the long-houses. The men would have cheered the wind by then, for they had drunk so much and were in a mood for cheering. Thorvard alone didn't cheer. He stood and grabbed his wife from her high chief's chair, and swung her around, his face so full of joy it almost seemed to glow. Then he held her high in his arms, and the crowd cheered again.

The men sang a drinking song after that, loud as a battle almost, thought Hekja. She and the women slipped indoors as the men grew drunker and the fights began.

"And let's hope no one has his legs chopped off this time," said Helga matter of factly to Hekja. But as she said the words Hekja heard Freydis raise her voice outside, calling a halt to the fights and drinking.

"For we depend on each other here," she cried, "our duty is to live, not die, like heroes."

Freydis ordered the fire banked down for the night after that. She and Thorvard went to bed in their curtained room, and the couples went to their bed closets, and the men climbed to the attic. Hekja could hear them laughing upstairs, and fighting still, but nothing much, in case Freydis should hear.

Snarf was lying by the fire, chewing a deer bone, and Hekja was combing her hair with the brush Freydis had given her, before she plaited it for the night, when the ladder creaked. Snarf looked up. Someone was coming down from the attic.

"Arf," he barked, but softly. He wagged his tail, too. It was Snorri.

"I wanted a mug of water," he said. "I'm thirsty after all that ale."

Hekja nodded. She put the brush down and began to divide her hair into braids. Snorri dipped a mug into the water barrel, then sat on a bench and watched her in the faint glow of the coals.

"Did you like the song?" he asked at last.

"Yes," said Hekja, paying attention to her plaiting and not to him. "But I think it was a pity you didn't let the swan sing, as well as the hero."

Snorri smiled at that. "True," he said. "Swans are supposed to be wonderful singers. Is it my fault they rarely let humans hear them?" He took another sip of water, and then said softly, "If you had been the swan, what would you have sung?"

Hekja did look at him then. "I think her song would have said, 'You are a prince, and I am a swan, and two people so different can never be happy together.'"

Snorri looked at her seriously. "Maybe they would discover that they were not so different after all."

Hekja shrugged, trying to seem as if she didn't care. "Perhaps they'd be happy for a while. But then the prince would go back to his kingdom. And the swan would be alone."

"You didn't listen close enough," said Snorri gently. "In my song the swan and the prince go home together."

Hekja froze. He couldn't mean that she might go back to Norway with him? "Imagine his parents when their son brought them home a swan," she said tightly. "They'd be horrified."

"Until they heard her sing," said Snorri. "I think they would love her then, as he did. But yes, a swan would need courage to marry a prince."

"I think," said Hekja softly, "that they would be happier with their own kind, swan with swan, prince with princess. And when he got back to his castle, the prince would know it too."

"Is that how you would sing the song?" Snorri demanded.

Hekja nodded. "A lonely prince, far from his own kind, who falls in love with a swan because there's no one else to fall in love with. But when the prince saw the princesses of home again"—she shrugged—"he'd soon lose all interest in beaks and feathers."

"No!" cried Snorri. "That's cowardice! You're scared to risk—"

A voice from behind the curtain interrupted him then. "Will you be quiet out there!"

It was Thorvard. Snorri flushed and put down his mug of water. Hekja concentrated on her plaits as the ladder creaked as he went back upstairs.

* * *

After that Snorri spent more time with the Skraelings. Sometimes he was gone for days. When he was back, he spoke to Hekja politely, as he did to all the women. He neither avoided her nor sought her out. Nor did he sing again.

The days flowed into each other. Freydis's belly began to swell. She had to tie her apron looser, till finally one of the women made her a bigger one.

Pregnant or not, she was still in command. She had promised to bring her men to Vinland, and she had. She had promised riches, and they were there. She had dismissed Finnbogi. She had traded so well with the Skraelings that there were furs beyond imagining waiting to be taken back to Greenland.

Now the trees turned gold and red, brighter than any autumn colors anyone had seen.

"Even the trees are richer in this land," said Hekja as she stirred the rennet water into the fresh milk to start its journey into cheese.

One of the women smiled at her. "Gold leaves don't buy iron pots," she said, but she meant it kindly. The women were all older than she was, and they were freeborn, but they liked Hekja. Today they were making soft cheeses that would be ready in a few days, instead of taking months like the hard cheeses. The Skraelings loved the soft cheeses as much as the hard ones.

Suddenly someone stood in the dairy's doorway, blocking out the light. Hekja looked up, and there was Hikki. She had seen little of him lately. Freydis had him running south and north, spying out the land, but she had kept Hekja with her.

"Can you come?" Hikki asked Hekja abruptly.

Hekja put down the cheese wrappings. "Come where?" she asked.

"Somewhere," said Hikki mysteriously.

Hekja looked curious. "If Freydis looks for me," she said to the women, "tell her I have gone with Hikki, and will be back soon." Snarf hauled himself to his feet as the women looked knowingly at each other.

"Where are we going?" asked Hekja again, as soon as they were beyond the fenced fields of the camp. Hikki shook his head. "You'll see," was all he said.

They were climbing a hill now, down toward the lake. The wild vines hung thickly here, though their fruit had long been eaten by the birds. Down in the gully a stream ran through the bracken, smelling of autumn leaves. Small furry beasts chattered from the branches. Snarf woofed at them, and they chattered again, too high for him to reach.

"Here we are," said Hikki finally.

Hekja laughed and looked around. "Where is that? There's nothing here!"

"There will be. This will be my land," said Hikki solemnly. "I will build my house here, on this hill by this stream. My thralls will clear the timber, and plant my wheat and oats."

"Your thralls?"

Hikki nodded. "We will all have a share of the silver after next summer, when the furs and timber are taken back to Greenland and Iceland. Enough to buy thralls and tools and everything we need. All of us who came here first will be rich, Hekja. All of us."

"I see," said Hekja slowly. She sat on the leafy ground, her back to one of the great trees.

"Do you think you would be happy here?" said Hikki quietly. "I am a thrall now, but I won't be one next summer. In time I will be as rich as any man in Vinland. We belong together, Hekja. We understand each other."

"Do we?" asked Hekja softly. "I suppose we must. We come from the same land. We are both runners, both have known what it is to be a slave. It's just . . ."

"What?" asked Hikki quietly.

"I want to see my home," whispered Hekja. "My real home. I want to go back to my village."

"Why?" asked Hikki, more gently than she had ever heard him speak. "What is left of your village now?"

"I need to know!" cried Hekja fiercely. "The girls up on the great mountain survived. Maybe others did as well."

"Are the girls so dear to you that you will leave all this, to go back to them? To live in a stone hut, and eat barley cake and fish and kale? Think what a life we could have here! Furs for your bed and wheat bread on the table. All the meat that you can eat. Thralls to serve you . . ."

"I could never have a thrall!" cried Hekja.

Hikki shrugged. "Some people would rather be a slave than free," he said. "They like to have someone tell them what to do."

Hekja was silent, thinking of Gudrun. Then Hikki said, "Would you really prefer your village to this?"

Hekja looked around, at the tall trees in their brilliant autumn cloaks, the sea beyond, the golden beach, the waves that stretched from sand to sky. Was her village just an excuse, so she didn't have to give Hikki an answer?

"No," she admitted finally. "You're right—I wouldn't want to live there now. I don't know! Hikki, I promised Freydis I would stay with her for two more years. After that—if you still wish it—ask me then."

Hikki grinned. "I will still wish it! By then I'll have your house built, the fields cleared. Two years—yes, I can wait that long."

"I must go," said Hekja abruptly. "Freydis will wonder where I am."

They started down the hill, Hikki laughing and talking of the house that he would build, the storeroom here, the dairy there. It was as though he assumed that Hekja had said yes.

Hekja was silent. But she let Hikki hold her hand as they walked down the hill. And even when she saw Snorri watching, she didn't pull her hand away.

* * *

When the trees lost their leaves, there were finally cheeses in the storerooms again. The Skraelings had stopped coming to trade.

"Perhaps they move away in autumn," said Freydis.

Hekja shook her head. "Their village looked too substantial to leave every year. Snorri might know," she added, trying to say his name carelessly.

"Snorri has never been to their village," said Freydis comfortably. "Only on hunting parties. He hasn't seen any sign of them either." She shrugged. She had become more relaxed since her pregnancy. "They'll come back in their own time, I'm sure. Not that it matters. We have more than enough trade goods to fill our ships next spring. And then . . ." Freydis looked out, past the harbor, at the sparkling sea.

"Then what?" asked Hekja. But she guessed.

Freydis laughed. "And then our ships will bring back more silver than we have ever seen—and more ships, and more men, too. This is just a start, Hekja. My father founded one colony. By the time my child is grown, I will have villages all down this land. And maybe there are still more lands to be found."

To Hekja's surprise, Freydis put an arm about her shoulders, and gave her a brief hug. "You will tell your grandchildren you sailed with me, Hekja," she promised. "And by then you will be one of the first families of Vinland."

Each morning now Hekja's breath turned white as she went to milk the cows, and each night a giant log was dragged into the fire pit, to smoulder all night and warm the house. But Leif had been right. Even through winter here the grass stayed green, and the cattle and sheep stayed fat in their fields. There would be milk all through winter, it seemed, in this rich land.

Then, one morning, the Skraelings attacked.

Chapter 37

The Attack!

Snarf heard them first. Hekja rolled over on her furs when she heard him bark, then shut her eyes again. It was a "Hey, look who's here!" bark, not a, "Watch out! Danger! Enemies!" bark. Perhaps some of the men in the other longhouse were setting out on an early hunt.

Snarf barked again, more urgently now. He ran up to the big wooden doors as though telling her to open them.

"Do you want to go out? Wait a moment then." Hekja shrugged off her sleeping furs. She yawned as she crossed the silent hall, and pulled at the wooden doors.

Suddenly she froze. The gray river was black with Skraeling canoes, silent and purposeful. Their men were ready with arrows at their bows. "Skraelings!" she screamed.

"What is it, girl?" One of the men ambled past her out into the dawn. "Another trading party? A bit early, isn't it?" He blinked into the dim light, then realized what she had seen. "Thor's boots!" he yelled, scrambling back into the longhouse. "Attack! Attack! Everyone to arms! Attack!"

Freydis stumbled from her bedchamber. Already men were scrambling for their swords and shields and axes. "What is it?" she shouted.

"Skraeling raid!" someone yelled to her.

Hekja grabbed Snarf by the scruff of the neck and shrank back against the wall, to keep out of the way. Thorvard was yelling orders now. Freydis was the colony's commander, but she had never fought a battle or led a raid. The only battle she'd even seen was the accidental landing at Hekja's village.

Hekja bit her lip. Thorvard was a good man, but not a man that others followed. Could he lead them now?

Freydis gazed around, then picked up her skirts and ran out the door—ungainly as her belly was now so large. She was going to the other longhouse, Hekja realized, to warn them, too. An arrow landed on the door behind her. Hekja darted after her, but was caught in the rush of people pushing through the doors. She struggled through them, into the courtyard, and looked around for Freydis. Men were pouring from the other longhouse now.

Suddenly Hikki grabbed Hekja's arm.

"Come on! Run!" he yelled. "None of them can catch us!" Hekja shook her head.

"There are too many of them!" Hikki shouted. "Don't be a fool! Run!"

"Freydis . . ." began Hekja.

"You owe her nothing!"

"No!" cried Hekja.

Hikki hesitated, then sprinted across the fields toward the trees. Without her.

An arrow fell at Hekja's feet. Someone screamed—one of the women, with an arrow in her stomach. She doubled over, then fell to the ground. An arrow whizzed past Hekja's face, close enough to feel its wind. She heard the wet smack as it buried itself in a man's shoulder.

Another woman made to go back into the longhouse. One of the men grabbed her. "No!" he yelled. "You'll be trapped in there! Into the trees! You can hide up there!"

The women began to run after Hikki, lifting their skirts high so they could scramble through the bracken.

Hekja heard a long scream and turned and saw Hikki stagger forward a few steps, trying to get to the safety of the trees. Then he collapsed, the feathered arrow in his back.

Hekja hesitated, but then pushed forward to try to get to Freydis. Another rain of arrows showered all around. The Skraelings were out of their canoes now, but for the moment they came no closer. Why run toward the Viking swords when their arrows could kill them at a distance?

A Norseman crumpled to the ground, and then another.

"Hekja!" It was Snorri. He grabbed her, putting his body between her and the Skraeling bowmen, just as an arrow thudded into him, below his heart.

Hekja screamed as he slumped next to her. She bent to try to help him, but one of the men pulled her away. "Run," he yelled. "There are too many for us! We all have to run to the trees!"

"No!" Freydis stumbled from the other longhouse, her pregnant belly big before her. "Why do you flee, brave men like you?" she yelled. "You should be able to slaughter them like cattle!"

No one seemed to hear her. Hekja crouched on the ground, as though to shield the dying Snorri from more arrows. His eyes were open and he saw her, though there was blood trickling from his mouth.

"Run," he whispered. "Run."

"Harrrrrrrrrrr!" It was a wilder shriek than Hekja had ever heard. She looked up. The fleeing Norsemen stopped and stared.

Freydis shrieked again. She ripped her dress open, so the bodice hung down and showed her pregnant belly. She bent down and picked up a sword from a man crumpled at her feet, then slapped it three times against her naked breast.

"If men will not fight, then women must!" she called. "Hekja!"

Hekja blinked. Part of her lay there with Snorri. Snorri, who had sung of heroes . . . Suddenly she seemed to find herself. She grabbed Snorri's sword from his limp hand.

It was a big sword, too heavy for a woman. But Hekja held it above her head and could not feel its weight, and shrieked as Freydis did.

And then they charged.

A pregnant woman and a girl charged a horde of Skraelings, Freydis shrieking like a storm up on the mountain.

The Skraelings stopped. Perhaps, thought Hekja, they think we are enchanted and arrows can't pierce us. They are thinking there's no other way a pregnant woman and a girl could run at a band of warriors and show no fear. Surely it must be magic!

Was this what Snorri meant, she thought exultantly. Is this what heroes feel, the final exhilaration of battle before we die?

She heard a noise behind her. The Norsemen were running too. But now they ran toward the enemy, not away. The Skraelings picked up new arrows and began to fire. But now the arrows fell on shields, not flesh.

The men were overtaking Freydis and Hekja now. Thorvard flung himself in front of them, so his shield protected Freydis, too. His was the first sword that crashed into the enemy, but there were others with him. Axes chopped through flesh. The flow of arrows stopped. Arrows don't work when the enemy is on you. Wooden clubs are no match for swords and axes.

Hekja faltered, lost in the tumult of men and blood and weapons, too short to see what was happening. She was only conscious of Freydis panting at her side, still sheltered by Thorvard's shield.

Then the Skraelings were running back to the canoes, dragging their dead and wounded with them. There were just enough alive to speed the canoes back up the river, as silently as they had come.

Chapter 38

After the Raid

Freydis let the sword fall from her hand, as though she had forgotten it. Thorvard ran with the other men, after the fleeing Skraelings. Hekja stared at them, unable to believe that she was still alive. Then she ran back to where Snorri lay upon the ground.

He was still breathing. He must have pulled the arrow out himself when Hekja ran on with Freydis. Now he lay unconscious, his blood in a dark pool on the soil. Hekja pulled her apron off, then knelt by his side and began to press the apron against him to try to staunch the flow.

Freydis had lost the fire that drove her toward the Skraelings. She almost staggered now as she walked back toward the houses. Her face was white, and dark shadows had grown beneath her eyes. One of the women ran to help her, but Freydis shook her head. She fastened her dress again with shaking hands.

"Bring the wounded inside," she ordered, resting her hands for a moment on her belly. Her voice was hoarse but steady.

"What if they return?" someone called.

"They won't for now. I want the rest of you to bring the logs we cut for timber. I want a fence around the houses by nightfall, as high as three men and pointed at the top, so no Skraeling can climb over it. Drive each log deep into the ground and leave a gate that can be barred." She caught her breath, as though in pain, then added, "A lookout. Build a lookout, too. We will not be taken by surprise again." She walked awkwardly over to Hekja and peered down. "What are you doing, girl? Smelling him?"

Hekja looked up and nodded. "A wise woman told me that is how you can tell how deep a wound is. If it smells bad, the gut is pierced. If not," she bit her lip, "then he may live."

"Well?" asked Freydis more gently.

"Maybe he will live," whispered Hekja. "Perhaps the arrow was almost spent and didn't go too deep."

"I hope so," said Freydis coolly. "His family is important in Norway. They will be useful when we need to trade." She beckoned to two of the men to help Hekja carry Snorri indoors and did not object when Hekja commandeered almost every sheepskin in the house to make him comfortable by the fire.

People looked at Hekja differently now. Before they had listened when she passed on Freydis's commands. But now they obeyed Hekja's wishes too. Hekja was still a thrall, but none of the people there that day would ever think of her as such again. Hekja had run side by side with Freydis as they led the fight against the Skraelings. Now they did her bidding and, almost without realizing it, Hekja expected them to do so.

She cut Snorri's shirt away as gently as she could and bound the wound again properly with clean linen. Tikka had once shown her how to do it so long ago. But the best that she could do was stop the bleeding. There were no healing herbs here, like the ones the witch used back on her mountain. Perhaps the Skraelings knew of some, but she did not.

Outside men yelled and carried poles for the new stockade, and Freydis walked white-faced from group to group, checking that all was done according to her orders. Snarf followed Freydis for a while, but as the day grew hotter, he trotted back inside again and lay by Hekja. Her eyes were on Snorri, whose face was almost as white as the sheepskins.

At midday, Helga knelt beside her and handed her a horn of buttermilk. Hekja shook her head. "He can't drink it," she whispered.

"For you, not him," said the woman gently. "It has an egg in it. You need to keep your strength."

Hekja sipped without tasting, then realized the woman still sat beside her. "Hikki?" she asked.

The woman shook her head. "I'm sorry, Hekja. He is dead."

"I see." Hekja thought she should feel something,

some kind of sadness. But it was as though every emotion had been used up.

"How many more are dead?"

"Two. Thorhild Gunnarsdaughter and Njal Valgardsson. Three wounded—Ketil, son of Thorgeir and Thorkel Gilsson. And Snorri Skald."

Hekja thought of Hikki, his face glowing as he talked about his farm. "Bury Hikki up on the hill above the gully," she whispered. "It will be his land. Let no man take it for their farm."

The woman stood up. "Yes, Hekja. I will tell them."

Hekja finished the milk, then used some soft leather to sponge away the blood that seeped from under Snorri's bandage. She stared at him, as though storing up the sight to last her all her life. Then Snorri opened his eyes. For a moment he did not seem to see her. And then his gaze steadied, and he gave an almost smile.

"Valkyrie," he whispered.

Hekja frowned and bent closer to hear what he had said. "What is that?"

"The maidens who take dead warriors to paradise," whispered Snorri.

"I would rather live with a warrior here than carry off a dead one," said Hekja firmly, but her eyes were gentler than her words.

Snorri tried to smile, then grimaced instead. "Maybe you are a berserker then," he whispered.

"How is it that you sit with me now, when you scorned me before?"

"Because I saw you dead," said Hekja softly, "and knew my life was empty. Wherever home is, it is with you."

Snorri nodded drowsily. Hekja wondered how much he had understood. But there was happiness in his smile now as well as pain. And when he slept this time, somehow his hand was holding Hekja's.

Hekja beckoned Helga with her other hand. She came at once, even though she was freeborn.

"What's a berserker?" asked Hekja softly.

Helga smiled. She guessed what Snorri had whispered. "They are the greatest warriors of all. They dress in animal skins and fight with such ferocity that no one can touch them, for they are protected by Odin."[37]

Hekja shook her head. "Freydis and I were not dressed in animal skins," she said quietly.

Then Freydis screamed.

---

[37] The Greenlanders were mostly Christian now, but old beliefs and myths lingered.

Chapter 39

A Child Is Born

It was not a scream like the one that she had given before. This was a cry of pain.

Helga left Hekja and ran outside. The other women followed her. Hekja glanced at Snorri, to check he was still sleeping, then ran as well, with Snarf at her heels.

Freydis stood by the first tall posts of the new stockade, clutching her belly. At her feet was a pool of water and blood.

Snarf whined, frightened by the new smell. But to Hekja's relief, the older women didn't seem worried. They helped Freydis indoors and up onto her bed platform, and fetched fresh cloths. They warned the men to stay outside.

All day Freydis strained and gasped. But apart from that first scream, she made no other noise at all. Hekja divided her time between checking on Snorri and patrolling the stockade, to make sure Freydis's orders were carried out, then reporting back to Freydis.

Even as the sweat ran down her face Freydis gasped out instructions: "The . . . gate . . . must . . . be . . . as . . . high . . . as the . . . fence. A shield about the . . . lookout." Freydis strained again and clenched her hands. "To keep him safe from arrows. I want a . . . lookout . . . Now!"

Each time Hekja checked on Snorri, she found Snarf with his head on Snorri's furs. Snarf looked up as though to say, "Don't worry. I'm guarding him for you. Nothing—not even death—will get past a dog like me."

The shadows were thickening as Freydis's child was born. Freydis did scream then, but as much in triumph as in pain. Hekja fetched Thorvard—he had been trying to work on the stockade and listen for the sounds indoors too. He knelt beside Freydis and looked at the red face of his son.

"His name is Erik," said Thorvard. "Erik Thorvardsson." He glanced at Freydis, hoping the name would please her. But his wife didn't seem to notice her son had her father's name.

"I am glad he is a boy," said Freydis wearily. "It is so much easier to be a boy." And then she shut her eyes and slept.

* * *

Freydis was up and in command again the next afternoon. It was not what women did, but Freydis was not like other women, and there was no one in the camp to dispute that now.

She fed her son that morning, but let another mother nurse him as well. Snorri was also sitting up by now, though Hekja would not let him move much. Snorri let her order him about. He seemed half in pain and half amused.

That first day Freydis checked the stockade and ordered the men to build another, even wider than the first. It would include some fields as well, where the cattle could be brought for safety. She spoke to each man, praising his bravery, never mentioning that they were all about to flee till strengthened by her courage.

Freydis had ordered each of the dead a hero's funeral. Their graves would be marked out like ships with stones, as there were no spare ships to bury them with.

Hikki was buried on his hill, as Hekja had ordered. He had no possessions to be buried with, Hekja realized. He had died before he'd found the wealth and freedom that he dreamed of for so long. She sat by Hikki's grave after the others had left, and tried to grieve for him, and for what might have been. He deserved that, at least, and so much more. But her mind was too full of worry for others. For Freydis, but mostly, for Snorri. Instead of thinking of Hikki she found she was looking at the harbor, to see if the Skraelings were coming back. So she went back down the hill to see if Freydis needed help.

Freydis was still everywhere, checking this and ordering that. Hekja persuaded her to lie down again, and let the women change her bloody pads and bring her baby to her. Hekja would take her orders to the men. Finally Freydis beckoned Hekja to sit beside her while her baby fed.

She was silent for a while, stroking her baby's fine red hair. And then she said, "Why? Why should they attack us now?"

"Perhaps they were waiting until after harvest," suggested Hekja, "so they could take what's in our storerooms."

Freydis shook her head. "Then why trade peaceably for so many months? To go from friend to enemy in just a few weeks? No, something must have happened to turn them against us."

The baby was almost asleep now, though he still sucked at Freydis's nipple. Freydis gazed at him for a moment, then said, "Finnbogi."

Hekja shivered at Finnbogi's name. "What do you mean?" she asked.

But Freydis shook her head. "Tomorrow," she whispered, her face suddenly whiter than it had been before. "Tonight I am too tired."

* * *

Next morning Freydis ordered the women to bring her best dress, her chains of gold and brooches and bangles too. Hekja was to wear her other dress, the one that was not stained with blood.

Freydis looked her up and down, as though to make sure Hekja was dressed correctly. She smiled. Her face was still white, but the shadows beneath her eyes were not as dark as before.

"We must get you more dresses," she said. Freydis pulled the curtain aside, then they walked out into the main hall. The room was full of men, swallowing their breakfasts, and women bringing them horns of ale or slabs of bread.

"Listen!" cried Freydis.

The hall fell silent.

"Now I have a son!" called Freydis. Her voice was clearer than a bird call. "His name is Erik the son of Thorvard. I call on you all to witness that I have a daughter, too. Her name is Hekja."

Hekja gasped and stepped back, but Freydis grabbed her hand and held it high. When she released it, she lifted the heaviest of the gold necklaces over her head and draped it over Hekja's shoulders. "Today you are my daughter," she promised, and kissed her. "Hekja Thorvardsdöttir."[38]

Thorvard looked a bit surprised, then smiled and nodded. "Granddaughter of Erik," added Freydis,

---

[38] The ending *döttir* means "daughter." Adopting teenagers or adults into your family was much more common then; it was a way to make important alliances and ensure loyalty. Today we take it for granted that women take their husbands' names. This used to be the case only in England, where a husband legally had all his wife's property. In the rest of Europe, and Scotland, too, a woman kept her father's name, and

looking pointedly down at Snorri lying on his furs. "A heroine from a line of heroes."

Someone thumped their sword on the ground. Suddenly the room was cheering. Despite his wound, Snorri was cheering too.

As for Snarf, there was a haunch of venison by the fire and no one was paying any notice. He'd finished the lot before anybody thought to look.

---

could still own property after marriage. The English practice spread to Scotland, and then with colonists to North America and Australia. By 1800 the English style was fashionable in Europe, too, and it spread still further, till now the peculiar legal habits of a tiny island have affected women's names across much of the world.

Chapter 40

Finnbogi

In all this time no one knew what had happened to Finnbogi's camp. Had they been attacked as well? Perhaps destroyed?

Finnbogi's men had stayed well clear of Freydis's camp all summer. Now Freydis decided that she and Hekja would go and see how they were faring.

"No!" Thorvard banged his drinking horn against their bedroom wall. Its end shattered, and the skyr ran everywhere. "You're still too weak," he said. "I will go, with half the men. The others will stay here and protect you."

Freydis's face was white, but her mouth still looked determined. "Bodily strength has nothing to do with it," she stated. "If I take men with me, I admit that I need them. No, my daughter and I must go by ourselves. Our weakness is our strength."

"Woof," said Snarf, from the floor.

Freydis smiled. "And Ice Nose will accompany us," she added.

"His name is Riki Snarfari," said Hekja softly.

Freydis looked at her consideringly, then nodded. "Riki Snarfari will escort us," she corrected. "Who could have a better guard?"

"I will not permit. . . ." began Thorvard, then shook his head helplessly. It was courage of a different sort, she thought, for a husband to accept that the men would follow his wife, not him. "I'll make sure she rests," Hekja told Thorvard gently.

He patted her hand with his big clumsy one. "Thank you, daughter," he said.

Freydis's brisk manner lasted till she and Hekja were just around the bend of the river. Then she stopped. "I need to sit," she said quietly, and sank onto the ground.

Hekja knelt by her in alarm. "Shall I fetch help?"

Freydis shook her head. "Back there I had to be strong. I will need to be strong for Finnbogi, too. But just for a moment, let me rest."

They waited till a bit of color flowed back into her cheeks. They walked on, more slowly than before, and rested often. Finally they came within sight of Finnbogi's camp.

"Well," said Freydis, staring.

Hekja nodded. Finnbogi's camp was smaller than theirs, with no fields of animals or grain. Instead there was a high stone wall, topped with a palisade of sharpened stakes, and a lookout high above it all.

"So," said Freydis softly. "Finnbogi has known for a

while that the Skraelings were a danger."

Suddenly Freydis drew a breath. She pointed.

Two women knelt by the lake. For a moment Hekja thought they were the thralls Finnbogi had brought from his farm. Then she saw that they were Skraelings.

Hekja gasped. "Do you think the Skraelings have taken the camp?"

"No," said Freydis softly. "Those women are captives. Thralls. Look at their faces."

Hekja bit her lip. "Yes," she whispered. "Free women never look like that."

The women hardly glanced at Hekja and Freydis. One had scars across her face, not from a sword, but as though she had been beaten many times.

"State your business!" someone yelled. It was the man up on the lookout.

Freydis called out, "I am here to see Finnbogi!"

Hekja could hear the sound of sliding wood as the gate was unbarred. Then it swung open and they entered.

This camp was different from the one down on the river. The longhouse was small, and grass was worn to dirt by many feet. Flies buzzed about a great heap of deer guts that had been dumped by the store shed.

"Look," whispered Hekja. Over by the far wall was a cross between a cage and a storehouse. There were women in it, and girls, and boys too young to have a beard. All of them were Skraelings. They were there to be taken back to Iceland, Hekja realized, and sold as slaves.

Finnbogi walked toward them, tall and confident as ever. He looked Freydis up and down, then inspected Hekja, lingering on the gold chain that shone about her neck. He looked at Snarf, as though wondering if he was near enough to kick. And then he grinned at them like they were some kind of a joke. "Well?" he demanded.

"Not well, Finnbogi Throstsson," said Freydis calmly. "The Skraelings attacked us two days ago."

Finnbogi nodded, as though this was no surprise. His grin grew wider. "And you have come to beg for shelter?"

"No," said Freydis shortly. She added, "We saw two Skraeling women as we came in. I see you have more over there."

"My men need women," said Finnbogi carelessly.

"Then you should have brought some more," said Freydis.

Finnbogi laughed at that. "Why waste good ship space on women? We needed women so we found some."

"And have made enemies of the Skraelings for us all," said Freydis.

Finnbogi laughed at that. "There speaks a woman!" he cried. "This is our land, and if we have to kill a thousand Skraelings to make it ours and have their women serve us, we will!"

"The land is rich enough to keep us all. Can I persuade you to reconsider, and let the Skraelings live in peace?"

"Peace!" boomed Finnbogi, as though it was the most absurd thing he'd heard. His eyes were hard. "Peace? Skraeling men and women will bring as good a price as the timber or even better. They take up less room in the boats, too. Why sweat at cutting timber when you can harvest thralls?"

A woman stepped out of the longhouse then. She stared as Freydis stepped up to her. "Helga Mordsdöttir, will you speak to your husband? We need to—"

The woman sneered. "Do not speak to me, Freydis Ericsdöttir. I respect my husband, unlike some I know. Listen to your own man before you bother mine. We have a chance at riches here. Go away and do not bother us."

A girl child peered around her skirts. Finnbogi's baby daughter. The mother picked her up, still glaring at Freydis with contempt.

"But the Skraelings—" began Hekja.

"Who are you, thrall, to speak to a free woman?" cried Finnbogi's wife. Another Skraeling woman peered out the door, then ducked away from yet another blow.

"If your own man cannot capture thralls for you to earn you silver, do not come whining here!" added

Finnbogi's wife. She turned and disappeared indoors. Freydis watched her go. Her face showed nothing. Then she said, "Come," to Hekja, and began to walk slowly from the compound.

Chapter 41

A Decision

Nothing was said until they were around the edge of the lake again. Then Freydis let herself sag upon a rock. There was sweat on her forehead.

"Rest," said Hekja gently. "There is nothing more we can do now."

Freydis stared at the ripples on the lake, then out at the bare winter forest. "Red leaves," she said. "There were red leaves upon the trees, as though they knew that this winter would bring blood."

"But the trees will be green again in summer," said Hekja earnestly. "Maybe no more blood will be shed?"

Freydis shook her head. "The Skraelings are warriors," she said wearily, "as we are warriors. If men came and took our women, we'd fight till every one of them were slain. This is what the Skraelings will do to us. And Finnbogi will take more and more of them to serve him and to sell as thralls."

"But that is Finnbogi," cried Hekja. "Not us!"

"It makes no difference to the Skraelings. We are

guilty because they are our kin and we do nothing. So," said Freydis standing up, though Hekja could see how much the effort cost her, "we must do something."

* * *

Suddenly Thorvard appeared, with four men, carrying Freydis's chair. Freydis walked toward him, but Thorvard scooped her up and placed her in her chair. The men carried her back to the house, with Hekja walking on one side and Thorvard the other.

Freydis slept after that, while the wet nurse fed the baby. When she woke, she stayed on the bed and fed the baby herself, then called for Thorvard and had the curtain pulled.

It was night when Thorvard came out. The fire flared in the pit, as the meat dripped from its chain above. Bread was baking on the hearthstone, and porridge cooking in the iron pots.

Thorvard looked troubled. But he shook his head when someone spoke to him. He wouldn't answer, just took his meat and horn of ale and sat staring at the fire.

The women had made a small milk pudding, with eggs and dried strawberries soaked till soft. Hekja put some on a plate, with a slab of wheaten bread and a mug of skyr, and carried them in to Freydis. The other women never went behind the curtain unless ordered, but Hekja now went where she wanted.

Freydis had a blank, worn look, as though every

bone and sinew was too tired to carry on. The baby lay asleep in a carved cradle by the bed. Hekja had seen Thorvard carving the cradle this winter, polishing it smooth with a stone.

"Well?" asked Hekja, handing over the plate. "What have you decided?"

"Thank you," Freydis said. She stared at the food a moment, as though eating was a duty that had to be borne. Slowly she took up her spoon and swallowed. "I have decided that we have two choices. We can join with Finnbogi and try to wipe out the Skraelings. Or we can try to convince the Skraelings that we are not their enemies."

"But how can we do that?"

"Tomorrow," said Freydis quietly. "You will know it all tomorrow. Now go." She smiled a little. "Snorri will wonder where you are."

"Snorri knows exactly where I am," said Hekja dryly. She pulled the curtain behind her as she left.

Chapter 42

The Battle

The house stirred early the next morning. Everyone knew something would be happening today, but no one quite knew what.

Hekja slept next to Snorri now, though not as man and wife. Snorri was too weak for that and, anyway, the wedding was still to come. Hekja wasn't sure when she had agreed to marry Snorri, if she ever had, but somehow the whole camp assumed the marriage would take place, Snorri included.

Not that it mattered. Sometimes Hekja felt her life and Snorri's were like two great ropes that finally twined together. They were stronger than they had been apart. If Snorri was going to get himself shot by Skraelings again—or in any other of the dangers Vikings seemed to plunge into—she was going to be there.

Freydis had given orders for a wedding feast to be prepared, and Thorvard had explained the marriage contract to Hekja. Her new parents would give her a share in the expedition's profits, so she would come to her marriage a rich and respected woman.

Hekja slept wrapped in her cloak and Snorri slept wrapped in his, but Hekja was there if he needed anything.

Finally the curtains parted and Freydis emerged. She wore a man's round metal helmet today and carried a man's shield and battle-axe. She waited till all were quiet, then said, "Call the others here."

Someone ran to summon the other household.

Freydis looked at the faces before her without speaking. And then she said, "I ask only one thing this morning. Will you follow me?"

"Yes!" cried someone, and another man called, "To the gates of Ragnarok[39]—and further!"

Freydis didn't smile at that. She just said, "Not quite so far, perhaps. Each man must arm himself. For those who should have been our companions have betrayed us. They have turned the Skraelings into our enemies. They threaten our very lives in Vinland. And so . . ." Freydis gazed out at her followers. "And so we must destroy them, like the ship rats that they are."

Someone cheered then, and soon everyone joined in. Since the Skraeling attack, it seemed that every man in camp thought Freydis could get them to Greenland and back without a ship, or call the clouds to milk the cows.

---

[39] the battle at the end of the world according to Viking mythology

The cheers chilled Hekja, nonetheless. Somehow it seemed wrong to cheer killing, even if, as Freydis said, they had no choice. These men cheered like their blood was up. For the first time in months, Hekja remembered the horror she had felt at the destruction of her village.

The men began to straggle out, swords, axes, and shields in their hands. Snorri tried to struggle to his feet, but Hekja pressed his shoulder. "Don't you dare," she said.

"But . . ."

Hekja shook her head. "You will collapse before we leave the fields. And then I would have to stay with you, when Freydis needs me." She forced a smile at him. "I have my duty, and this is yours—to get well. I will tell you everything that happens later, I promise. We can make our songs together."

"Even with a Norseman?" Snorri teased.

"Even with a Norseman," said Hekja, and pressed his hand. "Snarf," she whispered, "stay. You're on guard." Snarf whined, and licked her hand. He knew something was happening. But he obeyed.

Then Snorri said, "I want you to have my shield. I'd give you my sword, too, but it could be taken from you, and used against you. But take the shield. I wish it could be my arms that shielded you instead."

Hekja nodded. She lifted the shield that lay beside him and followed Freydis from the hall.

Chapter 43

The Death of Honor

It was late when they returned. The women ran from the stockade to meet them. They called out, but fell silent when they saw their men's faces. Freydis was in the lead, carried by two men in her chair. Her arms were bloody. The men were subdued, not cheering and victorious. And none of them would meet Freydis's eyes.

Hekja walked next to Freydis's chair. She carried a girl child on her hip, her head buried in Hekja's hair, as though she was afraid to look beyond. There was blood upon Hekja's skirt and arms, and on the child as well. Thorvard walked behind them. There was a great cut on one arm, and it was roughly bound up in a sling. But he made no sign that he felt the wound.

The women went from man to man, checking that all were there. A few were wounded, but it seemed that Freydis had brought all her army back.

One by one the men slipped away, to wash or think or talk among themselves. Hekja followed Freydis into the house. She handed the girl to one of the women, with instructions to bathe the child and feed her, then nodded to Snorri as he lifted his head anxiously. "What happened?" he cried. "Are you all right?"

Hekja met his eyes. "I'm not hurt. I have to help Freydis, then wash. I'll tell you about it then." Snarf ran to her, sniffing, as though looking for any wounds. But Hekja ordered him back to Snorri.

Hekja went with Freydis to her curtained room and helped her take off her bloodstained dress and armor. She beckoned to a woman to bring cloths and water. Then she walked down to the riverbank and washed and washed and washed.

She would never feel really clean, she thought. But finally she knew that there was no point scrubbing any more. She couldn't stay away from the longhouse any longer.

She walked back slowly, feeling the night wind cold on her wet skin. Inside, the women were serving food and hot ale to the men. Hekja shook her head when someone offered her a plate. She checked on the child, who was now sleeping. Then Hekja sat by Snorri and took his hand. And only then did she begin to shake. Tears ran down her cheeks, till he struggled up beside her and took her in his arms.

Snarf whined and tried to lick her face. Finally she stopped crying. Snorri called a woman to bring her ale and fish, and made her drink and eat.

Finally, when the cup was empty, he said, "Tell me what happened?"

"So you can make a song?" whispered Hekja.

"So I can understand," said Snorri softly.

Hekja shook her head. "I don't understand. At times I think I do, but then I think. . . ."

"Tell me," said Snorri again.

Hekja tightened her arms around Snarf. And then she said without expression, "We marched to Finnbogi's camp. Most of our men hid in the trees. Then Freydis called out to Finnbogi that we were leaving Vinland. She said she wanted to hire his ship to take our goods back, in return for half our furs. Finnbogi believed her. He and his men came down to our ship to sail up here to inspect our storerooms."

"And then?"

"And then we killed them," said Hekja.

Snorri stared. "Without a legal challenge?"[40]

"Yes," said Hekja simply. "We just killed them. They suspected nothing, so they were easily killed. Then we went back, and killed the others. They didn't have their swords, or shields. There were many more of us."

"I see," said Snorri softly.

"Do you?" whispered Hekja. "There was so much blood. The whole place stank of blood, and so did we. Sometimes I think I will smell it for the rest of my life."

"I should have been there," said Snorri. "For good

---

[40] Under Icelandic law it was no crime to kill someone in a legal challenge, but if you killed them without that—or after sunset or took them by surprise—it was murder.

or evil, I wish I had been there to bear this with you."

"No. It is enough that one of us . . ." Hekja said no more. And then she said, "Then there was Finnbogi's wife, too."

Snorri frowned. "What about her?"

"The Skraeling women ran off, into the forest, and so did Finnbogi's thralls. I let the people in the cage out too. I hope they keep running till they are safe. I hope they run and . . ." Hekja bit her lip and continued more quietly. "Finnbogi's wife struck one of them when she tried to run away. She broke the Skraeling's arm, I think, but the Skraeling was still able to run. When all the men were dead, Finnbogi's wife waited in the house with her daughter, as though defying us to touch her. And no man would. So Freydis took Thorvard's axe," said Hekja calmly. "She killed her with two blows. And Finnbogi's baby daughter saw it all."

Snorri said nothing, just tightened his arm about Hekja's shoulders.

"Snorri?"

"Yes?"

"I never asked you before. I think I was afraid of what you might say. Have you ever gone a-Viking? Raided lands and killed?"

"I have fought," said Snorri simply. "In battle with enemies of my father. I have killed as well. But no, I have never gone a-Viking. Those I have killed have always been armed. I have never fought a man unlawfully."

271

"But you sing of heroes—" began Hekja.

"You've heard my songs. Have I ever sung of killing?"

Hekja shook her head. They sat in silence for a while.

"The worst is," said Hekja at last, "I don't know what I should feel. Those men had to die, so we might live in peace with the Skraelings. Finnbogi and his wife were evil. But then I remember what I felt this morning. It was as though Finnbogi's camp weren't people at all, just enemies to kill. And I realize that is how my village was destroyed. We were simply enemies, no longer people. I will always see the blood and hear the screams. I will see Freydis's face as it looked today forever in my dreams."

"Time," said Snorri softly, into her hair.

"What about time?" Hekja's face was buried in his shoulder now.

"Time will make it easier. When we are far from here."

Hekja took her face from his shoulder. "Are we going far from here?"

"Yes," said Snorri. "When spring comes, when the ice clears up in the north. We will go with the trading ship, to Greenland, then to Iceland, then to my home."

"But your family—what will they think when you bring home a thrall?"

"I will be bringing home a wife to be proud of, Erik

the Red's granddaughter, a heroine, a Valkyrie."

"Who was once a thrall," insisted Hekja.

"Who was once a thrall, as my grandmother was."

"Your grandmother?"

"An Irish thrall. Daughter of a chieftain, but still a thrall. Besides," said Snorri lightly, "you will be rich."

"Will I?"

"I imagine we all will be," said Snorri gently. "From the proceeds of this voyage."

They were silent for a moment. Then Snorri said, "I would like you to see my home. But we do not have to stay there. It is your choice. But I would like us to sing together. To the king, perhaps, and to other kings. To sing of all we've seen and heroes we have known."

"Even of this day?" whispered Hekja.

"Perhaps," said Snorri quietly. "Perhaps one day, when we have found the words and thought how best to say them."

They sat quietly after that, perhaps hoping that the other one had dozed. About them the men and women went quietly to their attic or sleeping closets. Finally Hekja whispered, "Perhaps it will be worth it. Perhaps we will have peace, and the Skraelings will be our friends."

"Perhaps," said Snorri.

Chapter 44

Leaving Vinland

At their wedding feast, Hekja and Snorri sang together. It was a song of love and happiness, and Snarf joined in the chorus with his howl.

But in late winter the Skraelings came again, this time with flaming arrows. They did not break through—there was water enough to put out the fires. But everyone knew there would be a next time . . . and a next. . . .

Snorri offered to lead a party to the Skraeling village, to try to negotiate a peace. But when they reached the old place, the houses had been burned, and the fields were bare. Finnbogi's men had been there long before, leaving a bitter legacy. There would be no more trading with the Skraelings. But now the seas were open. It was time for Snorri to go home, with the trading goods that would bring the colony wealth, and with his new wife.

Hekja stood with Freydis for the last time, while the final bales of furs were loaded onto the ships.

They were taking Finnbogi's store boats, for as Freydis said, no one else would use them now.

Freydis had made every person swear they would never tell what had happened, that everyone would say that Finnbogi's party had decided to stay behind, and that Finnbogi had sold his ships to Freydis. But no one quite trusted that someone wouldn't let the true story slip.

Freydis was still the leader. The men obeyed her, but they didn't love her as before. The slaughter of Finnbogi's men and women had gained them nothing, except riches. Perhaps for some of them, that was enough. Others would remember a fight that had no honor, how they killed their countrymen without a legal challenge, and slain a free Norse woman as well.

Hekja could not forget either. Vinland had given her more than she had ever dreamed. But now there were memories of blood and hatred, and Freydis's face as she wielded the axe against Finnbogi's widow. Perhaps, as Snorri said, it was best that the songs of heroes always happened a long time away.

Over by the longhouse the wet nurse was feeding baby Erik. Finnbogi's daughter looked on. Freydis had adopted the child, though the demands of defending the colony had left her little time for motherhood.

Hekja glanced at Freydis and found her smiling. "You have come a long way from the little thrall on the island village," she said. "And now you are going even further."

"It's Snarf's fault," said Hekja lightly. "Did I ever tell you how the witch gave him his name? She said he'd be a Mighty Rover. I accompanied him, that's all."

"Arf," agreed Riki Snarfari, sitting to scratch a flea.

"Maybe," said Hekja tentatively, "you will come to Norway one day. To trade next year's furs, perhaps."

Freydis shook her head. "No, my dear. Wherever I go from here, it won't be back to Norway. This is good-bye." She hesitated. "Even if we never meet again, you will always be my daughter. I will never forget that when the men ran from the Skraelings, you stood with me. You are a daughter to be proud of."

Freydis paused. "There is a song, not one of Snorri's. It says the life of a man is only what people remember. Perhaps that is true of a woman, too. If you ever sing of me . . ."

"It will be a good song," promised Hekja. And she thought, but didn't say: but it may take years to find the words. If heroes weren't careless of life—their own or other people's—would they ever be heroes? Who could understand, who wasn't there?

She embraced Freydis then. For a moment Freydis clung to her, as though she might ask her not to go. Then she stepped back and gave a laugh, almost like before.

"Good journey!" she called. "And if you see a cloud like a new land on the horizon, think of me, and all your family here!" Then she was gone, striding back to the longhouse, without waiting to see the ship sail.

"Hekja!" It was Snorri, striding down the path from the longhouse, a final bundle under his arm. He held out his hand, and Hekja took it. They climbed into the boat together while the men uncoiled the ropes from the deck.

The wind filled the big woolen sail, and sent it flapping. The ship creaked, the oars splashed deep into the water. They were all the familiar sounds that Hekja had thought she would never hear again.

She stood with Snorri at the ship's rail and watched the land recede: the golden beaches where she and Snarf had run with Hikki, the white-tipped waves, the longhouse where she had found love and family, the tall trees on the hill where Hikki lay. And slowly Vinland turned to clouds, then vanished from the horizon.

Chapter 45

A Song for Freydis

For a long time Hekja heard little from Freydis. The distances were so great, it could take years for a message to find its way from Vinland to Greenland, then to Iceland, and to Norway.

They were good years for Hekja. Her home was in Norway at Snorri's family estates, but most summers she and Snorri traveled. She had even been back to her old village. The girls had survived, and Tikka, and even Bran, though the wound had left him simple. He was married to Banna, and they seemed happy, in their hut by the sea.

The village was richer now, for Hekja brought them sheep and hens, and glass beads from Venice for her friends. She also brought two of Snarf's puppies, so there would still be dogs hunting across the mountains where he was born.

Snorri and Hekja sang for kings these days. One day, at the king's court in Norway, she met the trader. He was an old man, with a shriveled arm, crushed by an iceberg in a storm at sea. He listened while she sang one of her Vinland songs. Sometimes Hekja felt strange singing about running with Hikki and Snarf along the endless beach. Here she wore a silk dress, with rubies at her wrists and neck. She still had never sung of Freydis. Even now, her feelings were too complex to put into words.

After the song, and the congratulations, the trader asked Snorri if he might meet her.

"Vinland!" he said to Hekja. "I was down there, just last year."

Hekja started. "How are they all? Freydis? And the colony?" she asked eagerly.

The old man barked a laugh. "Colony? There's no colony there now. Ruins, that's all we found."

"No!" cried Hekja.

Snorri took her hand. "It doesn't mean that they're dead," he said quietly. "They may have gone back to Greenland. Or even to another place in Vinland, safe from Skraeling attacks. I'll contact my uncle, get him to send a ship to Greenland next summer. I'm sure we'll have news of them then."

"Of course," said Hekja numbly. She walked over to the palace window and stared out at the neat fields. She was trying to remember the smell of Vinland forests, the sound of Freydis's laughter or the look on her face all those years before, when she told a frightened thrall how the albatross soared across the world. Freydis, the generous, the ruthless, the visionary.

Suddenly Hekja knew that what Snorri said was true. And now at last she knew the song that she should sing for Freydis.

Somewhere, far from land, Freydis was still sailing, her eyes fixed on a great bird overhead, waiting for the clouds on the horizon that would be a new land, with jewels hanging from the trees.

Author's Note

This story is based on real events, told in the *Gräenlendinga Saga* and *Eirik's (Erik) Saga* about two hundred years after they happened. When the sagas contradict each other, I've chosen bits from each. In other places I have simplified events.

Perhaps no one in history has ever been described in two such different ways as Freydis Eriksdöttir. In one saga Freydis is a dutiful, courageous wife—I didn't make up the scene where she charges the Skraelings, nine months pregnant and sword in hand. In the other saga she is a villain, killing five women with an axe. I have assumed that both stories have some grain of truth.

We shall never know what Freydis Ericsdöttir was really like. There is no doubt she was an extraordinary woman. I suspect she has been lost to history mostly because the later male writers didn't know what to make of her.

Thorvard, Leif the Lucky, and Erik the Red (or

Eirik Raudi) were real people too, and the places they traveled to also exist. Hikki and Hekja are mentioned in the sagas as two Scottish runners who were taken on Leif's first voyage to Vinland, but nothing else is known about them. I have placed them on Freydis's voyage instead. Finnbogi, too, was a real person, but there is no reason to think he was a villian. I may have done a brave adventurer a real injustice.

No one is sure where Vinland is. Viking longhouse remains have been found at L'Anse aux Meadows on the Newfoundland coast. But the coast there doesn't fit the detailed descriptions of Vinland in the saga, and wild grapes don't grow there. The grapes may have been other berries that could be made into wine—or maybe Leif Erikson was boasting about the lushness of the new land, just as his father had called his icy wastes "Greenland."

But it is likely that the longhouse remains are from another Greenlander voyage, and Vinland is further south where wild grapes do grow and the winters are milder than in Newfoundland. Or maybe the weather was very much warmer for a brief period in the years when the Vikings traveled up and down the coast of what is now Canada and the United States, and the land was very different.

I have tried to keep the Vinland in this book close to the description in the sagas, rather than place it at any known bit of land today. The Skraelings are based on descriptions in the sagas and also from accounts of fifteenth- and sixteenth-century European explorers. However, cultures—and areas occupied by various Native American nations—would have varied enormously between about 1000 ad, when Vinland was "discovered," and the fifteenth century, and almost certainly changed even more in the next five hundred years as well.

And if I have only come within whistling distance of the truth, perhaps I have done no worse than the saga singers, all those centuries ago.

Dates No one knows exactly when Leif Eriksson and the others went to Vinland. It may have been anywhere from 987 to 1011 ad. Our only information comes from the sagas, which were written as entertainment rather than as an exact history (and were almost certainly rewritten for political and religious purposes, too), and like the other information in them, their dates can be contradictory. But very roughly:

- 982 ad: Erik and his followers are outlawed for three years in Iceland. Erik had already been outlawed in Norway.
- 986 ad: Erik leads twenty-five ships of immigrants to Greenland. Fourteen ships reach the new land, with four hundred colonists. The other boats sink or turn back.

- 1000 ad: Leif "The Lucky" Eriksson travels to Vinland, stays the winter, and returns again a year later.

- About 1002 ad: Freydis Eriksdöttir leads an expedition to Vinland to trade or colonize, or is a member of another expedition with her husband, Thorvard, and Erik's son Thorvald. The expedition returns a year or three years later, though in one version Freydis stays behind.